SNAKE IN THE GRASS

1·07

The other man wasn't sneaking up on Clint, but had his eye on Eclipse instead. Gripping a hunting knife in hand, he extended the blade toward the Darley Arabian's hind leg while eyeing the tendon running just beneath the horse's skin.

Clint could see the hungry glint in the man's eye as he stretched that blade out to do his damage to Eclipse's leg. Crippling that horse in the middle of such harsh terrain was a sneaky way to impose a death sentence on Clint.

Eclipse had been shifting around to get a look at what was creeping up on his hind legs when he pulled his snout upward to catch a glimpse of Clint dropping down in front of him. The Darley Arabian jumped away to let Clint land safely, which also brought his hind legs closer to Galloway's blade . . .

THE GUNSMITH

280

THE RECKONING

J. R. ROBERTS

JOVE BOOKS, NEW YORK

THE BERKLEY PUBLISHING GROUP
Published by the Penguin Group
Penguin Group (USA) Inc.
375 Hudson Street, New York, New York 10014, USA
Penguin Group (Canada), 10 Alcorn Avenue, Toronto, Ontario M4V 3B2, Canada
(a division of Pearson Penguin Canada Inc.)
Penguin Books Ltd., 80 Strand, London WC2R 0RL, England
Penguin Group Ireland, 25 St. Stephen's Green, Dublin 2, Ireland (a division of Penguin Books Ltd.)
Penguin Group (Australia), 250 Camberwell Road, Camberwell, Victoria 3124, Australia
(a division of Pearson Australia Group Pty. Ltd.)
Penguin Books India Pvt. Ltd., 11 Community Centre, Panchsheel Park, New Delhi—110 017, India
Penguin Group (NZ), Cnr. Airborne and Rosedale Roads, Albany, Auckland 1310, New Zealand
(a division of Pearson New Zealand Ltd.)
Penguin Books (South Africa) (Pty.) Ltd., 24 Sturdee Avenue, Rosebank, Johannesburg 2196,
South Africa

Penguin Books Ltd., Registered Offices: 80 Strand, London WC2R 0RL, England

This is a work of fiction. Names, characters, places, and incidents either are the product of the author's imagination or are used fictitiously, and any resemblance to actual persons, living or dead, business establishments, events, or locales is entirely coincidental.

THE RECKONING

A Jove Book / published by arrangement with the author

PRINTING HISTORY
Jove edition / April 2005

Copyright © 2005 by Robert J. Randisi.

ISBN: 0-515-13935-1

JOVE®
Jove Books are published by The Berkley Publishing Group,
a division of Penguin Group (USA) Inc.,
375 Hudson Street, New York, New York 10014.
JOVE is a registered trademark of Penguin Group (USA) Inc.
The "J" design is a trademark belonging to Penguin Group (USA) Inc.

PRINTED IN THE UNITED STATES OF AMERICA

10   9   8   7   6   5   4   3   2   1

ONE

"Where is he?"

The question echoed through the hot desert air like the shaking of a rattler's tail. The voice that had spoken it was drier than the parched ground and was shot through with something close to a snarl.

Pulling in a deep breath that still didn't manage to fill his lungs, the man who'd been asked the question struggled to come up with an answer. That proved to be harder than it seemed for two reasons. First of all, he knew that speaking out of turn could very well be a fatal mistake. Second, all the blood had rushed to his head after hanging upside down for the better part of an hour.

The man who'd asked the question stood with his head cocked to one side as he tried to keep his eyes focused on target. He was a slender figure dressed in simple black clothes. Weapons were scattered all about his person, including several blades, a .44-caliber Smith and Wesson pistol, and at least two smaller holdout guns. His head was covered by a bowler hat that was pulled down low enough to mask a good portion of his face as well. Although his face was smooth and clean shaven, that didn't take away from the cold, calculating directness in his gaze, which shot through the man in front of him like an arrow.

"Come on, Ellis," the clean-shaven man said. "Tell me what I want to know quickly before your head pops like a bubble."

The man hanging upside down let out his breath and quickly sucked in another. His hands were bound behind his back, but that didn't keep him from continuing to pull at the ropes. All he'd gotten so far for his efforts was a deep, bloody chafe wound around his wrists.

"I told you before," Ellis grunted. By this time, there was some desperation creeping into his voice that grew more pronounced with every word he spit out. "I don't know where he went. He came into town, stayed for a bit and then left. He never said where he was headed and nobody really asked. For God's sake, Mister Galloway, you've gotta believe me!"

"And why should I believe you?" Galloway asked. "So far, you haven't told me a damn thing. You expect me to accept that someone like that rides into your town, does what he did and then just disappears? That's bullshit, Ellis, and you know it."

Ellis shook his head so vigorously that it got his entire body swinging gently from side to side at the end of the rope. Curling up like a caterpillar, he twisted to try and raise his head to alleviate some of the pressure building up inside of him. His ears and face were both bright red. Even the act of breathing seemed to make his brains swell up within the confines of his skull.

The moment he saw some of the color in Ellis's face start to fade, Galloway smacked his hand flat against the man's forehead. That sudden impact caused Ellis to stop his squirming and allow his body to hang straight down from the rope once again.

When he let out his breath this time, the effort shook Ellis's chest and forced a few beads of sweat to drip from his forehead. Sweat came from his neck and body as well, trickling down over his face in a series of crooked streams.

"I've done this plenty of times, Ellis. One thing I can tell you is that you don't have much longer before things start to break. I'm sure you can believe me on that one. Your ankles start to pull apart. Your eyes will start to bulge from their sockets. So much blood will fill that head of yours that it'll start to crack. I'll bet you can feel that right n—"

"Texas!" Ellis shouted.

Galloway squatted down so he was closer to Ellis's face. "Yeah? He headed for Texas?"

"I know he mentioned something about West Texas." Clenching his eyes shut, Ellis strained to fight through the growing pounding that filled his head. Every thump of his heart was like a fist knocking against a water skin that was twice as full as it should have been.

"Go on."

Ellis could feel his eyes pushing at the back of their lids. His heart was beating faster, only making matters worse. "It was a while ago. I can't remember everything he said."

"I've got all night. I can wait for you to think it through." There was a grim humor in Galloway's voice. Extending his left hand, he pushed Ellis just hard enough to get him swinging a little more. "Unfortunately, I don't think you've got so much time left."

It was an odd sight, to say the least. Physically, Ellis was bigger than Galloway. He was taller and even bulkier, sporting thick muscles on his arms and chest. But hanging with his head a foot off the ground and his feet held in the firm grip of rope, the odds weren't only skewed in Galloway's favor, but they were positively stacked so Ellis had no hope at all.

Suddenly, Galloway gritted his teeth and reached down to grab hold of the front of Ellis's shirt. Pulling him up with a surprising amount of strength considering his slender build, Galloway nearly brought Ellis up far enough to alleviate some of his discomfort.

"I'm reaching the end of my patience," Galloway snarled. "Do you think I'm an idiot?"

Ellis's eyes widened and he shook his head in a way that looked more like he was trembling. "N—no! I don't think th—that at all!"

"Then why would you have me believe that you could meet a man like Clint Adams and forget about it? Do you think I've never heard of him?"

"Plenty of folk've heard of him. I just—"

"You just thought you could bluff your way through me and I wouldn't know any better. Is that it?"

"No!"

"Is he related to you?"

Ellis's face registered his confusion at the change of topic in an almost comical manner. "Um . . . no."

"Then is he your best friend?"

"No."

"Then why are you ready to die for him? Because if you don't think I'll kill you, you're too dumb to live anyhow."

"Oh Jesus."

"Yeah. That's right," Galloway said as he drew a blade from the scabbard at the small of his back and pressed the cool metal against Ellis's throat. "Maybe you'd better start saying that name because you're about to meet the Lord Almighty in a moment."

"He said something about heading to Texas."

Ignoring those words, Galloway dragged the blade across Ellis's skin without breaking it. "I bet if I make a little cut here," he mused, "all this blood will come gushing out like a dam broke."

"Cassie!"

"What?"

"Cassie Dawson! She comes into town every so often to stock up on fabrics and fancy threads that come in from California!"

"Either start making sense or I gut you right now."

"Just listen," Ellis pleaded. "She comes through here and we catch up on things. She and Clint Adams got to know each other a while back and she sees him when he comes through these parts."

"Does he care for her?"

"I . . . I guess. All I know is that she said that he might be coming through again soon."

"When did she say that?"

"A week or two ago . . . I think."

Fixing his eyes on the dangling man, Galloway asked, "And you just remembered this now?"

"Plenty of folks still talk about Clint Adams. I hear it all the time working behind a bar. Cassie comes and goes and talks like everyone else and she only mentioned him in passing."

Galloway could tell plenty about a man just by staring into his eyes. In his line of work, he might just live or die by making a proper call regarding his take on someone's character. Although he couldn't be sure about the latter part of Ellis's story, he was certain the bulk of it was true. Ellis was too scared to be a convincing liar.

"Where can I find this Cassie Dawson?" Galloway asked.

"She lives on a ranch about ten miles from here."

"And what about those fancy threads? Where does she buy those?"

Ellis's face froze for a second. Regret seeped into his features as he realized just how much he'd told. When he felt Galloway's blade press against him a bit more, however, he spat out, "The Gold Coast Boutique on Second Street."

Having studied the hanging man's face for a good couple of seconds, Galloway smirked and said, "See now? That wasn't so hard." Then, he turned on his heels and started to walk away.

After a few silent moments passed, Ellis started to get anxious again. "Hey! What about me?" he gasped as his breaths started speeding up.

Suddenly, Ellis felt a hand grasp him by the chin and jerk his head back until he could see nothing but the ground and a set of boots.

"I didn't forget about you," Galloway whispered before pressing the edge of his knife against Ellis's throat and making a quick slice across.

Blood sprayed out in a thick gush that fanned out so that the crimson wave was the last thing Ellis saw. As he passed on, his ears were filled with the thump of his heart as it emptied his veins into the dirt.

TWO

Clint looked down at the cards he was holding and couldn't have been happier. Some men waited their whole lives for a straight flush to be filled in after drawing two cards for it. Plenty of other men were real good at making their own luck and padding out their hands to make sure they got the occasional windfall like that.

In Clint's case, it had been neither of those things. He knew better than to wait for a piece of luck like that and he was never one to cheat at cards. The truth of the matter was that he'd been hoping to pair up his jack or ten of hearts or possibly make a flush. Instead, he'd been given something so good that he had a hard time keeping up his expressionless facade.

"See your five dollars," Clint said while tossing in his chips, "and raise another five."

The kid sitting across the table from Clint hadn't only been drinking all night, but he was also afflicted with a terrible case of being too young to bluff. Like most bucks his age, he figured he was slick enough to buffalo anyone in the room and tough enough to make any man flinch with a sideways glance.

That was a dangerous combination for a gambler.

For Clint, on the other hand, it was just another gift from above.

"Oh you'll raise, huh?" the kid said with an arrogant sneer. When he glared at Clint, it was more of an effort to showboat rather than do any actual studying of his opponent. "Well, I'll see your five and raise another ten!"

Clint let the kid make a show of flicking his money into the pot and then studied his own cards. In truth, he wasn't even looking at the sequential row of hearts because it would only make him break his cool exterior.

"I've got your raise covered, but let's bump it up another twenty." Looking up at the kid and then to the women sitting at the table behind the players, Clint asked, "That's not too high for you is it?"

The question was worded just right and spoken with just the right tone to nudge the kid's pride. Following Clint's direction perfectly, the kid looked around to the women as well and started puffing out his chest while plastering a smug grin onto his face.

"Too high?" the kid asked. "You can't scare or bluff me outta this pot." Glancing around at the women now that he had everyone's attention, he added, "Ain't nobody in here can beat me at any damned thing. And there ain't nobody around who can bluff Ted Lenders."

Clint saw that the kid was starting to get a few smiles but was too full of himself to realize that not all those smiles were complimentary. Just when he could tell the kid was about to posture a bit more for one of the ladies who actually bought his line of bull, Clint made his big play.

"Prove it," was all Clint needed to say.

Not only did those two words snap the kid's attention fully back to the game at hand, but they also acted like a quick jab to his inflated ego.

"You want me to prove it?" the kid asked.

"No. What I'd really like is for you to stop talking and play." Although Clint thought he might have gone just a bit too far, adding that extra bit of fire under the kid was just as much of a gamble as anything that had to do with the cards he kept or tossed away.

This time, the gamble couldn't have worked any better.

The kid looked as though he was about to explode. He actually started to fidget in his chair and look around as though someone else meant to lend a helping hand.

"All right then," the kid said after winking toward the blond woman who'd caught his eye. "I'll play. In fact, I'll knock your ass clean out of this game." With that said, there wasn't anything left for the kid to do except to push in every chip that had been stacked in front of him.

Clint leaned back in his chair as though the move had actually caught him by surprise. Taking a few deep breaths, he fed the kid's ego by checking his cards nervously and then counting his own chips with a worried expression on his face.

"What's the matter?" the kid asked. "Too hot for ya?"

The others sitting at the table had folded their cards after the second round of betting. Now, every one of them leaned forward as if they'd suddenly found themselves in the front row of a boxing match. Two professional gamblers shot Clint a knowing glance but kept the rest to themselves. A trim brunette sitting at Clint's left smiled and shook her head while running her finger along the edge of her wine glass.

Finally, after a long enough pause, Clint shrugged and pushed in all of his chips as well. "I might as well call. It's only money."

"That's right. And soon it'll only be my money."

Triumphantly, the kid laid down his cards and spread them in front of him. "Aces and kings. Beat that!"

"Damn, that's tough," Clint said, finally allowing himself to truly relax and enjoy the moment. "But I think I can manage."

Clint set down his cards face-up and leaned back to level

his gaze onto the kid's smug little face. He saw that cocky grin drop so fast that he could almost hear it thump onto the floor. This time, Clint didn't bother holding back his own smile too much.

"What the hell is that?" the kid grunted.

Looking down at the cards, Clint replied, "Looks like a straight flush to me." When he reached out to rake in his winnings, Clint pulled the smile from his face and didn't make a show out of it. The kid had done enough of that already.

One of the professionals at the table, a tall man wearing a gray suit and bowler hat, shook his head and knocked his knuckles against the table. "Well played, Mister Adams." Turning to the kid, he said, "Don't let it trouble you, boy. Happens to the best of us."

Clint could tell the kid was stewing worse than a pot that had been left on the stove for too long. Just when he was about to buy a round of drinks for the table, Clint heard the one thing he'd been hoping to avoid.

"What's the matter?" the brunette asked, dropping the straw that would break the camel's back. "Too hot for ya?"

Rolling his eyes, Clint groaned, "Aw, hell."

THREE

The man walked into the Red Rooster Saloon through the door, which was propped open by a half-full spittoon. Boards creaked under his feet, joining the creaks made by all the others that were walking about inside the place. It was a busy time of night for any saloon, which meant that most of the rest of the town was asleep or getting close to it.

There wasn't much sleep to be had anywhere near the Red Rooster, however. With all the shouting, singing and general hell-raising that was going on, it was all the man entering the place could do to hear himself think. Still, he was no stranger to places like that and made his way through the crowd with practiced ease.

Standing at slightly above average height, the man cut a fairly impressive figure. His face was covered in coarse stubble that made his dark, Mexican features seem even darker. Wearing his gun in plain sight, he walked with a confidence that showed he wasn't afraid to use it, and that was more than enough to keep the would-be troublemakers quiet.

Stepping into the saloon, the Mexican shifted his gaze about to take in everything he could until he got up to the crowded bar. He leaned in between two drunks and rapped his knuckles on the bar to get the barkeep's attention.

Although the barkeep obviously didn't like the impatient knocking, he kept his comments to himself once he got a look at who was calling for him. "What can I get for ya?" he asked.

The Mexican leaned forward so he could be heard over the ruckus that seemed to be brewing in the back of the room. "I'm looking for someone."

"We got plenty of someones in here. You got anyone particular in mind?"

"His name's Clint Adams. You heard of him?"

"Sure I have, but you might want to think twice about calling him out. I hear he's plenty fast with the iron."

"I'm not here to call him out, amigo. I just want to have a word with him."

The barkeep narrowed his eyes and sized up the Mexican. His expression made it plenty clear that he didn't think too highly of the other man's request or his intentions.

None of this was anything new to the Mexican. There were enough banditos tearing up the trails lately to make folks nervous. But that didn't mean that the Mexican was full of patience himself, especially not tonight.

"You know where he is, then I suggest you tell me," the Mexican said, pulling back the edge of his dusty cotton jacket to reveal the badge pinned to the front pocket of his shirt. "And be quick about it. I've had a long day's ride."

The barkeep snapped to attention and replied, "Always willing to cooperate with the law, Sheriff."

"I'm a marshal. Marshal DelToro."

"Right, Marshal. If you're looking for Adams, he's right back there. Him and some others have been playing cards for the better part of the night."

DelToro glanced toward the back of the room and spotted several card tables. Every one of them was filled with men hunched over their cards. To make matters worse, the smoke over the gamblers' heads was like a dense, bitter fog.

Starting to make his way through the crowd, DelToro sifted through the faces he could make out through the dark haze. He had a vague description in mind of the man he was after but soon came to realize that slightly less than half of the men he saw could fit that same description.

DelToro stopped and turned around to find the barkeep still keeping an eye on him. "Which table?" he asked.

Just as the barkeep was about to answer, his eyes grew wide as saucers and he ducked down beneath the bar. He was back up again in a moment but was not alone. He had a sawed-off shotgun with him and was already thumbing back the hammers.

Reacting on reflex, DelToro went for his gun. Before he could draw, it was obvious that the barkeep wasn't about to take a shot at him. Instead, the other man was looking at something over the marshal's shoulder. DelToro spun around just in time to see a tall kid grab hold of one of the card tables with both hands and flip the thing onto its side.

At that moment, surrounded by a bunch of men wearing guns at their sides and carrying bellies full of liquor, Del-Toro felt like he was standing in the middle of a powder keg that was set to blow.

"Aw hell," the lawman groaned.

FOUR

"You goddamn cheat!" the kid yelled as his face flushed with a mix of anger and embarrassment.

Clint had seen the blowup coming and had done his best to avoid it. He'd actually been doing a good job until the brunette at the table had gleefully dropped the last straw onto the wrong camel's back. Now, all that was left was for him to deal with the mess without spreading it around.

"Hold on, now," Clint said, keeping both hands open and in front of him where the kid could see them. "You got a bad turn of luck. That's all. Take your loss and learn from it. You want a drink? The next round's on me."

"I don't want no goddamn drink, Adams! I want you to admit that you cheated."

One of the professional card players at the table got up from his seat and spoke in a voice that stank of whiskey. "I've seen plenty of cheats in my day, boy, and he ain't one of 'em. One hell of a slick talker and damn good at cards, maybe, but he's no cheat."

"You're just saying that 'cause you're probably a cheat too. All of you is cheats! Every damn one of you."

Clint could have sat in his spot and talked to the kid all night long. Unfortunately, the younger man wasn't so inclined. He didn't even want to hear what Clint had to say next before his eyes narrowed and his face took on a cold, almost lifeless expression.

Clint knew that look only too well. It was the look that signaled the end of talking as well as the point of no return.

The kid was already in motion and made a better than average reach for his pistol. Before he could clear leather, he saw Clint leap out of his chair and come toward him still holding both arms out in front of his body. Clint lowered his head and thrust his shoulder forward at the last possible moment, catching the kid squarely in the midsection.

The impact of Clint's shoulder pushed all the wind from the kid's lungs in a single huff. He'd delivered enough damage to buy everyone else at the table a few precious seconds.

Sure enough, the other gamblers knew what to do with the time they'd been given and got away from the kid as quickly as their legs would carry them. Everyone moved, that is, except for the brunette who'd pushed the kid over the edge and into the brawl.

While everything in the saloon had gotten quiet when the kid pushed his table over, all hell broke loose once Clint made his charge.

At other tables, men were grabbing for the pots while others were trying to stop them.

Women were stepping back and trying not to get caught in the fray while those who were already mixed up in it were swinging and kicking to get out.

Bottles started to fly and punches were sailing left and right until the first, inevitable gunshot exploded through the air. With all the commotion, it was hard for Clint to tell where the shot had even been fired or where it landed. The fact of the matter was that he had more than enough to keep him busy.

The kid snarled some garbled curse as he angrily slammed a fist down onto Clint's back.

Absorbing the punch without even feeling much of it, Clint kept pushing forward with his legs while trying to keep the kid from reaching his gun. He made it a bit farther than he'd expected before Clint was overpowered by the younger man and pushed aside.

Other guns were being drawn throughout the room, but Clint didn't pay much attention to them. The only weapon that concerned him was the one the kid was reaching for at that moment. As soon as the kid's hand closed around the grip of his pistol, he spat out a profanity that was swallowed up by the chaos that had filled the Red Rooster.

Clint's hand flashed down to the modified Colt in his holster. His eyes were set firmly upon his target and all trace of doubt had been wiped from his mind. At that moment, there was nobody else around and nothing else happening.

All that Clint cared about was the young man in front of him and the gun in that kid's hand.

The Colt snapped up from its holster and was pointed at the kid in the blink of an eye. Clint shifted his aim slightly and pulled his trigger to send a gout of flame and smoke from the Colt's barrel. Lead whipped through the air and hissed past the kid's face.

Although the kid ducked down with a surprised look on his face, he didn't drop his gun. Before he could take his shot, however, he was swept up into one of the other fights that had branched off of the main one.

"Oh my god, Clint!" came a familiar, if somewhat frantic, voice.

Clint turned but couldn't find right away the one who'd spoken. After a moment, however, he spotted the brunette peeking up from behind the table that had been knocked over. He rushed over to her and knelt down to her level.

"Get out of here, Cassie!" Clint said, forcing himself to shout so he could be heard over the growing ruckus.

But despite the hell that had broken loose around her, the brunette shook her head. "Not on your life! This is the most fun I've had since, well, since the last time I saw you!"

Not allowing himself to stand still even for a second, Clint tried to keep up with everything that was happening while also talking to the brunette. "Fun? You think this is fun?"

"You're damn right I do! And here I thought I was just coming to town to pick up some sugar and flour!"

Even though he couldn't believe Cassie's smile was actually getting wider by the second, Clint couldn't help but feel his own smile growing as well. Cassie had that way about her. At least, she did whenever Clint was around. It was hard to believe that she was normally a quiet, respectable seamstress.

"Well, do me a favor and get the hell out of here before you get hurt," Clint said. "And I promise we can have some fun once we're out of here."

"Do you have the money?"

"What?"

"The money from the game," she said. "You won it. Go get it."

"Will you just—"

Clint was cut off when the kid reached over the side of the table and took hold of Clint by the neck with both hands. From there, he lifted Clint straight up until he was almost completely off the ground. It was all Clint could do to suck in a quick breath and grab onto the kid's arm before the life was choked out of him.

Just as Clint's vision was starting to blur around the edges, he saw a figure rush toward him with his fist cocked all the way back next to his ear. The kid was still doing his best to throttle him as Clint tried to escape from that arm that cinched like a noose around his neck. The more he struggled, however, the tighter the kid seemed to squeeze.

"Goddamn cheat," the kid grunted. "This'll show you."

That other figure was getting closer by the second. Clint

didn't want to kill the younger man unless it was necessary, but it seemed to be getting more and more necessary as Clint found it harder and harder to breathe. His boots slammed against the kid's legs with no effect.

Grudgingly, Clint went for the Colt just as that looming figure finally arrived and shot his fist straight out toward Clint's eye. His hand fumbled at his holster, which was enough of an error to cost him a precious fraction of a second. Now, finding himself still in a headlock with a fist speeding straight for him, all Clint could do was brace himself and prepare for the worst.

FIVE

The meaty fist came at Clint like a cannonball, but to him it seemed to roll in like a thundercloud that could not be stopped. He twisted as much as he could, but the kid's arm was locked in tightly around his neck and kept him from going much of anywhere.

In no time at all, the stranger's fist was set to land squarely on its target. Clint's eyes clenched shut even tighter as the fist sailed right past his head and slammed into the kid's face behind him.

The impact rocked the kid back, loosening his grip on Clint's neck in the process. It took a moment for Clint to realize that he was then free, but then his reflexes took over until the rest of his brain caught up.

The man who'd thrown the punch was a burly Mexican with rough features and a weathered snarl on his face. He shook his hand and winced before turning his attention toward Clint.

"You'd be Clint Adams?" the Mexican asked.

"I sure would."

"I've been looking for you."

"Then let's save the rest of the introductions for later. We've got a bit of a mess here."

Clint saw some movement coming from the corner of his eye and twisted around to face it. Surprisingly enough, the kid was trying to shake off the effects of the punch he'd taken. That entire side of his face was red and swelling up already. Every step he tried to take was shaky at best.

Reaching out to take hold of the front of the kid's shirt, Clint pulled him forward so he could make sure he was heard above everything else going on. "Take this as a lesson, kid," Clint said. "Either learn to play poker better or learn to be a better loser. You'll live a whole lot longer."

It was uncertain how much of Clint's words got through. Somewhere along the line, the kid was pulling himself together and working himself up again. Before he could put anything behind the snarl forming on his face, the fire in the kid's eyes was put out for good when Clint delivered a solid uppercut to his jaw.

That punch snapped the kid's head back and dropped him straight to the floor. Blood trickled from the corner of his mouth, but his chest rose and fell as though he was just having a bad night's sleep.

"He'll have one big headache, but he'll be all right," the Mexican said. "Come on. It looks like the locals can finish up this mess."

Sure enough, when Clint looked around, he saw that what scuffles were still going on were being handled by saloon workers or a few men wearing badges. That left only one other loose end that Clint needed to tie up before leaving The Red Rooster.

"Cassie?" he shouted. "Where are you?"

Although the brunette wasn't where he'd left her, Clint quickly spotted her at the bar with an empty bottle in her hand. He rushed over there and pulled her away from a pair of rowdy drunks before she could put her bottle to use.

"Let's go before you start any more trouble," he said.

Cassie was all smiles as she set the bottle on the bar and

allowed Clint to drag her away from the two drunks. "Just trying to help out," she said.

"I think you've done plenty."

"Don't tell me you're forgetting how to have fun. I thought you were the wild one."

"And I thought you could handle your wine a little better. It's time to get some coffee into you."

Once she'd fallen into step alongside Clint, Cassie wrapped both arms around him and pulled him closer so she could plant a kiss on him that nearly knocked him over. Even though he was trying to move her out of the way before she got caught with a stray punch or flying chair, Clint could feel her responding to him as though they were alone in bed.

Her breath came in deep gasps and her hands moved over him with building intensity. Only after they got outside did Clint allow himself to try and defuse the fire that she was stoking. He didn't have to do much more than give into the moment, in much the same way that Cassie was doing. To that end, Clint wrapped his arms around her and returned the kiss with enough added fire of his own to quench her thirst.

Breathless, she moved back and showed Clint a wide smile. "Now that was fun," she whispered.

Clint returned the smile and shook his head. "You know how to keep busy, that's for sure." Turning his attention to the man standing close by, Clint shrugged and extended his hand. "Sometimes it's better to go with the tide rather that try to paddle upstream. I appreciate the helping hand back there."

"More of a helping fist," the Mexican replied. "And it was no problem. I could tell you were taking it easy on that boy."

"Yeah? Well it sure didn't feel too easy when he was squeezing the life outta me. I never did catch your name."

The Mexican closed a solid grip around Clint's hand before replying, "Miguel DelToro."

"Good to meet you, Miguel." Just then, Clint's eyes caught a glimpse of something beneath the fold of the Mexican's jacket. He reached out and pushed aside the lapel to get a look at the badge lying underneath it. "Or should I call you Marshal?"

"Marshal?" Cassie asked as she took a closer look at DelToro's face. "You're not the town marshal."

Before the Mexican could speak for himself, Clint explained, "He's not town law, Cassie. He's a U.S. marshal."

"A federal man, huh?" she said with an approving nod. "That sounds like an exciting job."

DelToro nodded and straightened his jacket. "It can be. Especially on nights like this one. Is there somewhere a little more quiet where I can have a word with you, Mister Adams? I don't think it'll be too much longer before some of those cowboys get tossed out here."

"There's a little restaurant a block or two from here," Clint said. "They might be closing up about now, but I should be able to convince them to let us in."

As Clint started walking down the street, Cassie walked arm in arm beside him. The further they got from the Red Rooster, the more Cassie seemed to revert into a quiet, reserved girl. Her dark hair was still strewn carelessly about her face, but her eyes were now downcast and all traces of the wild smile that had been there before were gone.

"You know something, Clint?" Cassie said. "I still say you should have taken the money you won. Maybe we should go back and get it."

Clint and DelToro looked at each other in disbelief.

"I think there's been plenty of excitement for one night," Clint said.

She looked up at him with an unmistakable allure in her eyes. "Oh, I don't know about that."

"Is that the restaurant you were talking about?" DelToro asked hopefully.

The place was a small storefront with a dim, flickering light coming from behind a set of clean white curtains covering a rectangular window. Only a small shingle hanging in front of the door marked the place as a restaurant and not one of the many little shops along the boardwalk.

Clint nodded. "That's it."

As the trio walked up to the front door, they were greeted by a wrinkled face peeking out from behind the curtains. At first, the old woman looked annoyed. As soon as she spotted Clint, however, she smiled and stepped back so she could get to the door.

"I hope you weren't about to close up," Clint said as the door opened.

"For you," the old woman said, "I can stay open a bit longer. Come in!"

SIX

Compared to the Red Rooster, the quiet restaurant seemed like a paradise. Apart from Clint, Cassie and DelToro, the place was empty. The air smelled like coffee and dinner rolls. The only sound to interrupt their conversation was the clanking of pans against the stove and the occasional swinging of the kitchen door.

"They seem to like you here," DelToro said to Clint.

"I eat here a lot."

"And you eat a lot of steaks," Cassie added. "For breakfast and dinner."

"That too." Accepting the water and bread that was set in front of him by the old woman, Clint didn't even have to place his order for her to know what he wanted.

The other two ordered their meals, sending the old woman to hurry off and prepare them. Before getting to the kitchen, she locked the door and drew the curtains tightly so nobody else walking by would get the wrong idea. Del-Toro watched her with a bit of nervousness that didn't go unnoticed.

"What's the matter, Marshal?" Clint asked. "She's just making sure nobody else walks in to keep her here any later."

"I know. Old habits die hard, though."

Clint nodded and studied the Mexican. He had a look about him that wasn't uncommon in soldiers and lawmen. There was a wariness in his eyes that came from seeing too much blood. There was also a tension in his muscles that came from so many years of constantly being ready to spring without warning.

"Someone after you?" Clint asked, speaking quickly and directly to try and catch the lawman off his guard.

"No," DelToro replied. "There's someone after you."

This time, it was Clint who'd been caught off guard. He recovered quickly and sipped his water to wash away the uncomfortable feeling that was creeping up on him. "There's usually someone after me. Why should that concern a U.S. marshal?"

Although DelToro started to reply, he paused and took a look at Cassie.

The brunette was sitting in her chair, as proper as could be, straightening her hair while looking into a small hand mirror that she'd taken from the purse hanging from her arm. Once the talking had stopped long enough for her to notice, she looked away from her mirror and then at the two men who were now staring at her.

"What?" she asked, self-consciously. "What's the matter?"

"Would you mind giving us some privacy, ma'am?" DelToro asked.

"Is this a matter of secrecy?" Clint asked.

"No, but it might be best to make sure that not too many others hear what I have to say."

"Just spill it, Marshal. It's been a long night."

"All right then." When DelToro took a breath, he seemed to do so more to get over his annoyance with Cassie looking on than any sort of nervousness. "Do you recall meeting up with a killer named Galloway?"

"Is that his first or last name?" Cassie asked.

Keeping his focus on Clint, DelToro said, "That's the only name he goes by."

Clint thought it over and then shook his head. "Can't say as I do."

"Well he remembers you well enough. In fact, he's been tracking you down for the last couple months or so. At least, that's as long as we've been aware of it."

"Which brings me to my original question. Why would the U.S. marshals be aware of something like this?"

"Galloway started off as a gun for hire, but he's branched out into much more than that. He's been taking money to kill politicians and cattle barons as of late, and local sheriffs can only chase him so far until he moves into another jurisdiction. That's where I come into it."

Now, it was Clint who seemed more than a little uncomfortable. He kept glancing over toward Cassie until finally he reached over to put his hand on her arm. "Maybe you should get going," he said to her. "I don't like the way this is sounding so far and the less you're involved, the better."

The last couple of minutes had been enough to bring Clint and the brunette straight out of the mood they'd been in after leaving the saloon. Although Cassie tried to maintain her fun-loving smile, it was plain to see that the wine she'd drunk was no longer having much effect.

She nodded and put her mirror away. "All right, but promise me you'll come to see me before you leave this time. I want to say a proper good-bye."

"I will, Cassie. Thanks."

She got up and gave Clint a quick kiss before heading to the kitchen to cancel her order. After a bit of insistent arguing from the old woman, Cassie waited for another minute or two before leaving with a plate of food covered in a linen napkin. She waved to both men before heading out the door.

"She seems like a good woman," DelToro said. "A bit of a handful, but a good woman."

Clint chuckled under his breath and nodded. "You've got that right."

Just then, the old woman came out to place a plate of food in front of each man. She refilled their coffee and water before heading back into the kitchen.

Clint's steak was delicious. He knew that before biting into it because he'd had a steak from that restaurant every day since he'd arrived. DelToro picked at his own food grudgingly at first but then started digging in once he got a taste of it for himself.

"I can see why they know you so well here," the marshal said. "I'd probably come here enough for that too if I lived around here."

"So what else do you know about this Galloway?" Clint asked. "You say I'm supposed to have met him before?"

DelToro nodded. "That's a fact. One of the other men tracking him did some checking on his history. It seems Galloway has been a respected man in his field for some time. Just over a year ago, he was hired to set his sights on you."

"Where was this?"

"A town called Wescott. It's not too far from here."

Nodding, Clint said, "I remember going through there a couple of times. There was some trouble, all right."

"I figured that would shake something loose for you. Do you recall someone taking a shot at you? It was probably from a distance, since that's the way Galloway likes to operate. Word has it that you spotted him and fired off a round before he could kill you."

"It's coming back," Clint said as he worked to chew a tender piece of steak. "Looking back, I recall dealing with the trouble and taking care of the men out to kill me, but so many of the faces just seem to blend together."

"That's not too surprising. Galloway made his reputation as a sharpshooter, so you might not have even seen his face."

After swallowing, Clint smirked and shook his head.

"What's so funny?" DelToro asked, unable to keep himself from smiling as well.

"After all the years I've been riding from one end of this country to the other, looking back on something like this seems like I'm just looking back on a normal day's work. It just amazes me how much a man can get accustomed to."

DelToro nodded and shook his head. "I know exactly what you mean."

SEVEN

The two finished their meal without having to say much of anything else. Both of them could sense something familiar about the other that commanded more than a little respect.

For Clint, he could see that DelToro was a solid type of person and a man of action. What he'd seen in the Red Rooster had been more than enough to convince him of that. But more than just the marshal's skills in a fight impressed Clint. It was a bit early for him to stake his life on that assessment, but Clint had kept himself alive this long among dangerous people by being a good judge of character.

DelToro had been going through the same process of sizing up the man in front of him. As he ate, he thought about what he already knew and compared it to what he'd seen. So far, he couldn't come up with anything to make him feel ill at ease.

By the time the old woman came out to clear the plates, both Clint and DelToro were more relaxed. Once the bill was settled, they left the restaurant and started walking down the street.

It was late enough by this point that they were the only two souls to be seen in the immediate vicinity. Their steps against the boardwalk sounded like fists knocking on the door of an empty room. Faintly, the sounds from the saloon district made their way to this more respectable part of town.

"Sounds like they're still going at it," DelToro said, nodding toward the rowdy voices and rambunctious music.

Clint nodded. "You can bet on that. It's probably best I got out of there when I did. Too bad, though. It's been a pretty relaxing couple of weeks since I've been here."

"Sorry to be the one to put that to an end," DelToro said genuinely.

"Don't flatter yourself," Clint replied. "Something always comes along. At least this time it's coming from someone not out to kill me."

DelToro took a few more steps and said, "How do you know I'm not out to kill you?"

"Same way I knew that kid in my poker game was full of shit. Two kinds of men wear a badge, DelToro. There's greedy men and there's real lawmen. You're a real lawman, so stop trying to test me and say what you came all this way to tell me."

DelToro laughed a bit under his breath. If he was talking to any other man, he might have thought that Clint was full of himself. But he knew better than that. Otherwise, he wouldn't have even bothered seeking him out.

As if reading the marshal's thoughts, Clint asked, "Why have you come to talk to me? You've got to know that I can take care of myself and don't have much need for a federal escort."

DelToro chuckled and fished a cigar from his shirt pocket. Clenching the cigar between his teeth, he got a match and struck it against the side of a darkened building as he walked by. "I'm not here to escort you, Adams. I'm here because you've done plenty of favors for the U.S. marshals and it's not our policy to leave good men like yourself high and dry.

"This man that's hunting you down is more than just a

killer. He's a goddamn epidemic. He's been getting messy simply because he likes it and because he knows he can get away with it."

"If you and your men know so much about him, why don't you just bring him in?" Clint asked.

The cigar blazed in front of DelToro's face, lighting his features as he pulled in a breath and dimming once he let the smoke curl out from his mouth. "It's not that simple. We know his work and can tell where he's been, but only by picking up the pieces when he's through. He's a monster, but he's also damn good at what he does."

"So what have I done to warrant all this special attention?"

"You really don't remember?"

Clint shook his head.

Smiling, DelToro looked up at the stars and let out a genuine laugh that set his belly to shaking. "Oh Jesus," he said between breaths. "I'll bet that would piss Galloway off even more if he knew that." Looking away from the sky, he said, "You took his finger, Adams. His right trigger finger. It was one hell of a spectacular shot but real devastating to a man who fires a gun for a living."

Clint's eyes narrowed and he felt the memories flow into him in a rush. "I was finishing up that business in Wescott when the lead really started to fly. Hired guns were coming at me from every direction. I figured out I was being herded to a certain spot and just barely spotted him in time to draw and take my shot."

"From what I hear, most men wouldn't have had time to do more than blink, but that sounds about right."

Clint was talking to himself as much as he was to Del-Toro, running through the chain of events while they were still in his head. "He was standing in the dark, so I didn't have much to shoot at. All I did was aim for the glint of light that came from his gun and then shift a bit off from there."

"Like I said before, one hell of a shot."

Realizing that no more memories were going to hit him just yet, Clint shrugged and said, "I guess it was. I thought I'd killed him."

"Well, it would've worked out better all around if you had. He dropped out of sight for a while and then came back with a vengeance."

"He just needed some time to shift to his new style, is all."

"That's right. And once he did, he started making enough big kills to catch our attention. He was good at sneaking around before, but now he's like a ghost. In fact, Galloway has been a busy man lately," DelToro said. "He's gotten his touch back for killing. Only now, he just has to work up close since he's not too good of a shot anymore. He's also been making enough money to hire some people to work for him. From some of the kills he's made, he's either building himself a nice little network of spies or has grown eyes in the sky."

"Sounds like he's been prospering just fine since our last run-in."

"There's just one problem. Anyone who watches Galloway for more than a few hours can tell he's not quite dealing with a full deck."

"Yeah. Aren't all murderers a bit off in their thinking?"

"This is different. Galloway has recovered from his injury. I'll bet he could get enough work to save up and buy his own little town south of the border and live there for the rest of his life."

"But he won't do something like that."

"No. He won't. He's too busy chasing you down and working himself up to face you again."

"I'm not exactly hard to find, Marshal."

"We got a hold of one of his spies not too long ago," DelToro said. "He told us that Galloway has built you up to be the devil himself and is waiting for the perfect time to kill you. He wants his spies to get close to you but not lay a finger on you. He insists on it."

"Sounds like he's afraid."

"He's crazy is what he is, Adams. You'd know that if you ever met up with him." Laughing under his breath, DelToro added, "If you met up with him, the Lord only knows how crazy he'd get."

"I don't have to know him to know that he won't stop killing. Men who have killed that much are either defending themselves or they've gotten a taste for blood."

Glancing over at Clint as they walked, DelToro studied the other man with a bit more scrutiny than before. "Sounds to me like you know a lot about Galloway after all. Looks like I made the right decision to come and find you, señor."

"If you found me, then you can find Galloway," Clint said. "He's bound to slip up sooner or later. You're already dogging his trail pretty good by the sound of it."

"We are. And if we had more time, I'm sure we could catch him. But he's getting twitchier by the day. He's even started getting his own hands dirtier than usual by torturing and killing anyone who can point him in your direction. It's time to put an end to it before he kills you or anyone else. It's time to put an end to him."

EIGHT

Cassie felt like she was walking on air, even after her pulse had slowed and the ringing in her ears had died down. The more she thought about the brawl in the Red Rooster, the more she wanted to turn back around and find Clint so she could keep her heart racing.

The smile on her face grew and she developed a spring in her step that bordered on a skip. She knew she might have looked a bit foolish just then, but she didn't care. She felt too good to care about such things as appearances. After all, her normal life was still waiting for her once she got back to her needle and thread.

Still thinking about the Red Rooster, she took one more step and then pivoted around to look back in the general direction of the saloon. While she was too far away from the saloon to get a look at it, she was able to see something else.

Actually, she could see someone else.

That someone was at the other end of the street and stopped dead in their tracks when they realized they'd been spotted.

Cassie turned so she was facing in that direction and squinted a bit into the darkness.

"Hello," she said in a friendly voice that echoed down the empty street.

Taking a few backward steps, she kept her hands clasped behind her while waiting for a response from the other figure. The figure started walking toward her.

The other person's steps were slow and deliberate. Even though some sounds from the adjacent streets drifted through the air, the silence in the immediate area took precedent and hung over Cassie like a cloud.

"Beautiful night," Cassie said, twirling around so she could look where she was walking. Although she was still moving with an excited spring, her steps were quicker now. In fact, she started to feel an urgency pushing her along the street and away from the dark figure.

Her blood was racing again. Part of that was out of excitement and part was out of fear. In Cassie's present state of mind, however, one melted right into the other to give her a flutter in her stomach that wasn't entirely unwelcome.

Whatever pleasantness there was in the sensation wasn't enough to keep the fear back for long. The more that grew, the quicker her steps became.

When she reached the end of the street, Cassie could see light from the busier districts reaching out toward her. Without buildings closing in on her from either side, she felt as if she'd reached some sort of haven. That boosted her confidence enough to turn and take another look at what was behind her.

She practically jumped from her skin when she saw that the figure following her was now twice as close to her as the last time she'd checked.

That lean figure was close enough for her to see the line of a jacket as well as the hands stuffed into its pockets. The shadows still clung to the figure like ink, making it hard for her to see much else in the short time she allowed herself to stare.

"I know the marshal's on patrol right about now," Cassie

said with as much strength as she could put into her voice at that moment. "Is that you?"

The figure didn't answer. In fact, it didn't even move.

"No? Well, I'm sure the law's around here somewhere." Despite all her efforts to maintain calm, Cassie was unable to keep the tremble from sneaking into her voice. "If that's who you're looking for, I'm sure they're not too far away."

She'd added that last part more to help her own spirits, but Cassie's tone wouldn't have fooled much of anyone. It didn't even sound convincing to herself, which was why she turned her back on the figure and started walking even faster toward a street that was more well lit.

The next street over wasn't exactly brimming with activity, but enough businesses were open later so that more lighted lamps lined the boardwalk. No matter how quickly Cassie moved toward those lights, she didn't feel as if she was making any progress.

She could feel the eyes of the other person boring holes into her back. Every stray crunch of dirt or rattle of a loose pebble echoed in her ears until she found herself running toward a man who'd just stepped out of a small theater.

"Good evening," Cassie said to the man in a quick, grateful voice. Her smile was a bit too wide as she rushed toward the man, which caused him to step back a bit into the doorway.

"Uh . . . hello," the man said as Cassie rushed toward him.

Cassie forced herself to laugh and turn at the last moment to avoid knocking the poor man off his feet. Reaching out to brush her hands over him, she was ready to hang on for dear life as she turned to check the street behind her.

Her stomach clenched and she held her breath, making that simple backward glance seem like the final step over the side of a cliff.

The street was empty.

Seeing that was like feeling the touch of a guardian angel's hand on her shoulder, and it took all of the dread from

Cassie's heart. When she looked back at the man she was holding, her smile was practically warm enough to cast a glow upon his face.

"Sorry about that," she said as she took her hands off the man after dusting off his shoulders. "Didn't mean to frighten you."

The man tipped his hat, welcoming the smile as well as the attention he was getting. "Not at all, ma'am. Would you like me to walk you home? Can't be too careful this close to the saloon district."

After taking another glance around, Cassie shook her head. "No, I should be fine. Besides, I don't have much farther to go anyway."

"Suit yourself."

With that, Cassie pointed herself in the direction of Clint's hotel and started walking.

Quickly.

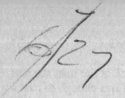

NINE

"I don't mind helping out the marshals," Clint said as he leaned against a post and hooked his thumbs through his gun belt. "But I'm not an assassin."

The two men had come to a stop on a corner where they could put their backs to a solid row of storefronts and be able to keep watch on everything around them. Neither one had needed to say when to stop. Both had instinctively picked out the perfect vantage point.

DelToro was savoring his cigar. Holding it between thumb and forefinger, he took it from his mouth and studied the softly glowing tip. "We want to take Galloway in," he said carefully. "But if he won't come in quietly, then so be it."

"Dead or alive, huh?"

"That's the way it stands at the moment, señor. If you knew more about Galloway, you'd understand."

"Oh, I understand just fine. I still don't see why you need me. There's plenty of marshals out there as well as plenty of other freelancers who are better suited to this task than I am."

"But Galloway isn't after them, Adams. He's got his sights set on you."

Clint smirked and nodded while slowly turning his head to look at DelToro head-on. "I was wondering how long it would take to get down to the bare bones of it."

Shrugging, DelToro said, "I've laid my cards out this whole time. You've met up with Galloway before and you've done good work with the U.S. marshals in the past. Galloway has a way of sniffing out when he's being tracked."

"But there's more to it than that," Clint said. "Get on with it."

After DelToro placed the cigar between his teeth, he drew in a deep, smoky breath that caused the tip of the cigar to flare brightly in front of him. The glow of the burning tobacco cast a dim red light upon his features. Once the glow faded, DelToro exhaled a thin stream of smoke.

"We're prepared to pay you five hundred dollars for taking this job," the marshal said. "If you bring in Galloway, you get to collect the bounty being offered for him."

"That's very generous. The *Federales* have never paid that much that I know of."

"It's a dangerous job."

"They all are." Clint paused, looking across at the marshal as though he was trying to figure out if he was holding a full house or a busted flush. The lawman was a tough one to read, however, but that didn't stop Clint from going with his own instincts.

"You want me as bait," Clint said, watching DelToro carefully for his reaction. "That's what all this is about, isn't it?"

The lawman's face didn't give away a thing. "That's a bit harsh. I think of it more as preparing you for a storm that's headed your way."

Clint smirked and looked around the street. There were some others walking by, but they were just moving into or out of one of the nearby watering holes. "This Galloway is after me, so you figure that if I get out there a little farther, he'll come running. Is that why you offered that extra five hundred?"

"That's a fee for your help. It's a bit more than we usually pay, but that's just because we're not exactly making a very reasonable request." DelToro looked Clint in the eyes when he added, "He's not the same man you met up with before.

"From what I've seen of his handiwork and heard from the few people he's left alive, Galloway is anything from loco to possessed. Whichever one you chose to believe, he is dangerous and unpredictable and wants nothing more than to see you dead, Adams. There's no doubt about that."

"Oh, I don't doubt it." Clint shifted his gaze skyward. "There's plenty of killers who get that same idea."

"Look, you don't have to take the job," DelToro said. "If I was in your place, I wouldn't want any part of it. But Galloway needs to be stopped before he does any more damage. I wanted to talk to you personally because you've saved the lives of some other marshals that happen to be friends of mine. Anything you do from here is up to you, but Galloway is coming for you either way. We're doing our best to get him but . . ." DelToro let the sentence fade with a shrug.

Clint was still studying the marshal carefully. It would have made things easier if DelToro seemed like a snake in the grass, but that simply wasn't the case. The Mexican was tough as nails, to be sure, but there wasn't anything about him that struck Clint as peculiar.

"Who else is on this job?" Clint asked.

"If you want someone along for the ride, that can be arranged."

"You'd be willing to let me work alone?"

DelToro actually looked surprised by that question. "Sure," he said. "Why wouldn't we?"

"How close has Galloway gotten to me?"

This time, DelToro did flinch a bit before responding.

"Actually, I don't know about that. We only caught one of his spies and that was on another case, but he mentioned tracking you was one of his best paying jobs. That means there's surely others. As for how close any of them got to you at any time, I really couldn't say."

"So he could be here?"

After taking a moment to think that over, DelToro shrugged. "Could be, but I doubt it. After that scene in the Red Rooster, he would have found you and taken his shot by now. Then again, Galloway has gotten harder to predict with every passing day. Who knows what a crazy man thinks?"

"Can I think it over, or do you need an answer now?"

"I can give you a day," DelToro said. "After that, I need to get moving. We are still tracking him on our own as well."

"All right then," Clint said. "I'll meet you here tomorrow."

"*Bueno.*" As he started to walk away, DelToro stopped and glanced back over his shoulder. "Do me a favor, Adams. Watch your back."

TEN

Clint was still thinking about DelToro's offer when he opened the door to his hotel room and stepped inside. It had been a hell of a way to end one hell of a day and Clint was just glad the whole thing was over. Several years ago, knowing that a killer was out for his blood would have been upsetting to Clint. Now, it was an all-too-familiar fly in his ointment.

"If you think you're getting any sleep tonight," came a voice from the dark, "then you've got another guess coming."

Recognizing the voice instantly, Clint shut the door behind him and said, "Do any of your customers know how you like to spend your nights, Cassie?"

"My customers are a bunch of gossiping women who haven't stepped foot out of this town in years." Leaning forward so some of the moonlight filtering in through the window fell over her naked skin, she added, "Of course they know."

"Well, after tonight, I'd bet they're going to be awfully proud of you."

Cassie was laying on her stomach with her legs curled up behind her. She was sprawled across Clint's bed, easing closer to him as her dark hair spilled over her back. "Tonight's been wonderful, Clint. I never thought I'd be in the middle of a fight like that."

"In the middle of it? Seems like there wouldn't have even been a fight if you weren't there. I may be known for plenty of things, but throwing punches in a saloon isn't really one of them."

Cassie put on a pouting frown as she reached out to take hold of Clint by his belt. Pulling him closer, she sat up until she could put her hands on his shoulders and look him in the eyes. "Are you mad at me?"

Back in the Red Rooster, Clint would have had a much different answer to that question. Looking down at her trim, naked body silhouetted in the pale light put him in a better frame of mind. There was still an excited fire in her eyes that seemed to go beyond what she wanted to happen on that bed.

"You're something else, Cassie," Clint said, unable to let himself get mad at her. "I'll give you that much."

Her pout shifted quickly into a hungry smile and her hands quickly got busy working at unfastening his belt buckle. "Actually, I was thinking that you could give me something more."

Clint moved his hands over the top of her head, sliding his fingers through her hair as she unbuckled his gun belt and dropped it to the floor. Her eyes grew wide for a moment at the sight of the gun but then shifted back to the growing bulge at his crotch.

"I hope I wasn't too much trouble tonight," she whispered while taking off his pants and pulling them down.

Clint was in the process of unbuttoning his shirt as he replied, "To tell you the truth, I had a hell of a night."

Reaching up to rake her nails gently along Clint's bare chest, Cassie didn't stop until her hands were gripping him by the hips. "It's only going to get better from here," was all she said before leaning forward to wrap her lips around his cock and slide him all the way into her mouth.

Clint had been unable to guess how hungry she was for him until now. Cassie took every inch of him into her mouth and moved her head back and forth along his length. Just when he'd managed to catch his breath, Clint felt her tongue begin to slide along the bottom of his shaft before swirling around it in smooth circles.

The moonlight bathed Cassie's skin in its pale glow, accentuating every line of her body as she slowly writhed on the bed in front of him. Her hair brushed over her shoulders as she bobbed her head. Her upper body shifted as she alternated between grabbing hold of him and the edge of the bed.

Her spine was a gentle line that traced delicately down to the tight, rounded curves of her buttocks. When she looked up at him, Cassie's mouth glistened with moisture and her tongue eased out to tease him one more time.

Moving on pure impulse, Clint reached down to pull Cassie to her feet. She came away from him reluctantly but then gave in with an excited smile as he practically lifted her off the bed. She moved forward to accommodate him and wound up kneeling at the edge of the mattress with her breasts pressed up against Clint's bare skin.

Clint could feel her erect nipples pressing against him just as he could feel the way Cassie trembled with anticipation as he ran his hands along her back. Her skin was smooth and cool to the touch, making it seem as though he was caressing moonlight itself when he felt her. Touching her naked body took him to a better place.

Some men drank whiskey. Clint wasn't much of a drinker, so he didn't turn his nose up at any chance to get his mind off the things lurking in the darker corners of his world.

Cassie rested her head on his shoulder and felt her muscles relax the moment Clint's fingers found them. "That's so nice," she purred into his ear.

But Cassie wasn't about to get comfortable just yet. Her

body was slowly writhing against his, quickening Clint's pulse until he could no longer hold himself back. His hands moved over her hips and tightened around her buttocks, pulling her close as he started moving her back farther onto the bed.

Cassis locked her arms around him and hung on, allowing herself to be positioned onto the middle of the bed. When Clint moved on top of her, she spread her legs willingly until she felt his erection brush against the smooth lips between her thighs.

Lingering there for a moment, Clint savored the way she looked beneath him. Her hair was splayed out over the bed and she watched every move he made as if she was studying her intended prey. When Clint made a move toward her, Cassie's eyes widened and she pulled in a quick, expectant breath.

Clint moved closer, pushing his hips forward until the tip of his cock eased partly inside of her. Leaning down, he placed a lingering kiss on the side of her neck and pushed inside of her just a little bit more. He could feel her heart pounding inside of her as well as her nails digging harder and harder into his back.

"I swear you're trying to torture me, Clint Adams."

"After what you put me through tonight, I'd say you deserve it."

Cassie couldn't exactly argue on that point. Instead, she pushed her head back into the mattress and savored every tingle that Clint sent through her.

ELEVEN

The place where DelToro was staying looked more like a bunkhouse than a hotel. There was no sign over the door and certainly no welcome mat out front. All that could be seen was a long, narrow building that looked sturdy enough to weather another storm or two before collapsing beneath its own weight.

DelToro walked to the building and kept right on walking until he'd gotten to the back door. A few of the windows along the side showed some signs of life, but even that was nothing more than a few flickering candles or the occasional shifting shadow.

One of those shadows moved to the door at the back of the building where DelToro was standing, quietly finishing off his cigar. When the door opened, DelToro looked casually in that direction. He only needed that much of a glance to know who was there.

"Evening, Bill," DelToro said. "A bit late for you, isn't it?"

Bill Lockley was a stout bear of a man. He walked with a swagger and had a look about him that made most others get out of his way from pure reflex. The others who didn't feel such reflex still got out of Bill's way just to keep from getting trampled.

Lockley was the town law in Brigham Way and had been for over ten years. He ran things the way he saw fit and didn't take much advice or guff from anyone else. His light brown hair was kept cut short beneath a large hat. He was usually clean-shaven, but this night his face was sprouting a thick crop of coarse stubble.

"Just because a man doesn't prefer to stay up till the break of dawn doesn't mean he's not able. Besides," Lockley said, "you're not exactly looking fresh as a daisy either."

"I just got back from the Red Rooster."

"You were at the Rooster? I don't suppose you were responsible for all the commotion?"

"Nope."

Lockley glanced at the cigar DelToro was smoking and then gave the U.S. marshal a steady gaze. He kept that gaze locked in place until DelToro finally reached in his pocket and pulled out another cigar. He handed it to Lockley who eagerly took it from him.

"Much obliged," Lockley said. When he reached into his pocket, he had to push past a row of his own cigars to get to a match. Noticing the critical look on DelToro's face, Lockley shrugged and said, "What can I tell you? You *Federales* get paid a hell of a lot more than a simple town marshal."

Lockley lit his match and then put flame to his cigar. He puffed a few times, rolled the smoke inside his mouth and exhaled. "So, did you find what you were after?"

"You could say that."

"Adams or Galloway?"

"Adams. He was in the middle of that scrap at the Rooster."

Lockley nodded. "Then at least I know I've got that Lenders boy locked up for good reason. I heard that the kid and some other fella started that brawl. If that other fella was Adams, it had to be the kid that threw the first punch."

DelToro listened to the other lawman but didn't really pay much attention. He had too much else on his mind to worry about problems that didn't even fall within his job description.

"I suppose you had a word with Adams," Lockley said.

DelToro nodded. "Yeah."

"Then I also suppose you and him will be heading out of my town soon." Noticing the look he got from DelToro, Lockley shrugged. "You worry about your jurisdiction and I'll worry about mine. Adams is a good fella, but his type draws too much heat to a place. And seeing that you're after a killer like Galloway doesn't make you much of a welcome sight either."

DelToro couldn't help but laugh at the town lawman. Lockley had a way of speaking that made it perfectly clear he didn't care much what others thought. "I know I'll be leaving soon, but I can't speak for Adams."

"Then maybe I should have a word with him. You know, just to make sure he's not of a mind to start any more trouble."

A few more puffs and DelToro's cigar was down to a nub. He took it from his mouth, flicked it to the ground and then mashed it with the heel of his boot. "I appreciate you letting me stay here for the night, Marshal."

Lockley shrugged. "That's what these quarters are for. You *Federales* and the occasional soldiers that pass through."

"Well, thanks all the same. I'll be sure not to overstay my welcome."

Stepping aside so DelToro could open the door into the bunkhouse, Lockley waited until the Mexican was just about to enter before asking, "Did you tell Adams everything?"

DelToro paused, his hand on the door and one foot inside the building. "I told him everything he needs to know."

"Damn shame if you ask me. Ask a man to put his life

on the line to help you out and you can't even be straight with him."

Wheeling around, DelToro looked the other man square in the eye. Although the Mexican was bulky in his own right, he wasn't able to get Lockley to back up even half a step. The fire in his eyes did manage to wipe away some of the smugness on Lockley's features.

"Don't stand there and talk to me like I'm doing anything wrong," DelToro snarled. "If even half the stories are true, Adams can take care of himself and anything that comes his way. I've got men getting killed going after this animal Galloway and if there's any chance of getting someone like Adams to help then I've got to take it."

"And I'm sure he would have helped regardless. I know plenty of other lawmen who've had their fat pulled from the fire by Adams. It's just the . . . well . . . the other part that may make things a little tricky. That is, if Adams were to find out."

"And that's why I didn't tell him. This plan has to go just right or it won't go at all." DelToro winced as though his own words had stung him.

Lockley took another puff from his cigar. "This is your plan, DelToro. I won't get in the way, but I'm sure as hell glad I'm not a part of it."

There was plenty the U.S. marshal wanted to say to that, but he kept it all to himself and went in to try and get some sleep. He knew it wasn't going to be an easy task.

TWELVE

Cassie was on all fours, grabbing hold of the headboard with both hands while Clint entered her from behind. Her back arched every time he slid into her and she slowly tossed her hair from side to side. As their bodies fell into a rhythm, she began to moan louder and louder.

Holding onto her hips with both hands, Clint massaged the firm slope of her buttocks before moving his hands up over her back. When he reached up as far as her shoulders, he could feel her tightening around him as she tossed her head back to look at him.

"Oh God," she said. "Right there. Don't stop."

Clint placed his hands on her shoulders and took hold so he could pull her forward while slamming his cock deeply inside of her. As their bodies made contact, they both let out a moan that echoed throughout the room.

Remaining still inside of her, Clint felt his erection grow even harder. She must have felt it too, because Cassie looked at him over her shoulder while letting out a smooth, low purr. Now, she was the one who started moving back and forth, easing herself toward the headboard and then pushing back against him.

Clint savored the view he had from where he was kneel-

ing. Cassie's skin was slick with perspiration and the air
smelled like sex. Her hair stuck to her neck and back in
thick strands, giving her even more of a feline appearance
as she clawed at the bed and ground her hips wantonly
against his body.

Reaching forward with one hand, Clint took up a thick
bunch of her hair and pulled her head back just enough to
see the wide smile on her face. Her eyes were closed
tightly, but when Clint pumped vigorously into her, they
fluttered open soon enough.

Every muscle in her body was taut. When he reached
around with his free hand to cup her breast, Clint found her
little nipple to be surprisingly hard. The more he pulled her
hair and rubbed her nipple between thumb and forefinger,
the more Clint could hear her moans getting louder and
louder.

Suddenly, Cassie pulled the headboard so strongly that
it seemed she was going to break it in two. Her pussy
clenched around Clint's shaft and her breaths came in a series of quick bursts. Her orgasm swept through her like a
storm, leaving her body limp for a few moments as she
slowly turned to look at Clint once more.

"Jesus," she whispered.

Before Clint could make one more move, Cassie had
pulled away from him and was turning around to face him.
Her naked, sweaty body was like a sight from a dream. The
unashamed way she moved in front of him only made it
that much more tempting to him.

She knew exactly what she was doing to Clint and
smirked mischievously as she repositioned herself. "Now,"
she said while placing her hands on his chest and pushing
him back, "it's your turn."

Clint allowed her to shove him down until he was laying
back upon the mattress. From there, Cassie slowly climbed
on top of him, taking her time to move her hands and legs
along every part of him she could reach. As her fingers slid

through the hair on his chest, her legs brushed against his thighs until she was straddling him.

The moonlight silhouetted her body perfectly, glistening off her skin and making the room feel even hotter than the desert had a right to be. Her pert breasts swayed slightly as she shifted on top of him until she was poised just above his cock.

With one hand, she took hold of him and guided it to her slick opening. Cassie lifted herself up on her knees until she was able to lower herself down again, enveloping him within her. She let out her breath slowly until he was all the way inside. Only then did she close her eyes, lean her head back and start to rock gently back and forth.

At first, her hands remained upon his chest. Once Clint took hold of her hips and guided her momentum, Cassie straightened her back and pressed her hands against her breasts. Rubbing her nipples with a steady flicker of her hands, Cassie began to sway and moan with building pleasure.

Clint reached around with both hands to cup her tight backside. Kneading her flesh within his grasp, he pumped his hips up and buried his cock inside of her. Every time he did, he could see her stomach tighten as she pulled in a quick breath. When he slid out again, she trembled slightly and rocked her hips along the hard shaft of his penis.

Waiting until he could feel his own climax approaching, Clint slid his hands along her thighs, down to her knees and then back again. As his fingers moved upward, he traced a path along the insides of her legs until they grazed the moist thatch of hair between them.

Cassie opened her eyes and looked down at him like she was dizzy. Just as she started to talk, Clint's fingers found the sensitive nub of her clitoris and rubbed it with a fleeting, flickering touch.

That stole the breath right out of Cassie's lungs and she moved her hands along her body until she was bracing them against her knees. That was the only thing that allowed her to stay upright as Clint continued to thrust into her while massaging her in just the right spot.

When Cassie opened her eyes again, there was an almost animal hunger within them. She leaned forward and grabbed the mattress on either side of Clint's head. Now, she rode him furiously, thrusting her hips back and forth while taking every inch of him inside of her.

Clint wasn't able to massage her any longer. He was barely able to keep from being pushed off the bed as Cassie rode him for everything she was worth. He wrapped his arms around her, found her new rhythm and then adjusted his own movements to fit it.

After that, they were soon able to spark an orgasm that shook both of them at the same time. Cassie's fists clenched tightly around the sheets while she leaned down to press her mouth against Clint's neck.

Clint pumped once more into her body and exploded within her, moving only slightly after that until he couldn't move any more.

They were so spent that Cassie didn't even bother getting off of him. She fell asleep right where she was laying and stayed there until Clint finally shifted her onto the bed beside him. He started to doze off as well but was awoken by the breathy, exhausted sound of her voice.

"Thank you," she whispered.

Clint laughed a bit and said, "That sounds odd coming from you right now. Especially since you were the one to drive me out of my mind."

She smacked him lightly on the chest. "I'm not thanking you for that. I'm thanking you for putting up with me. I know I can be a handful sometimes."

"Sometimes? Try all the time."

"Only all the times I'm with you. After you leave, I'll go back to sewing and wishing to be wild again."

"If you're planning on saving that wildness up when

I'm gone, I'll try not to stay away so long. Otherwise you might just kill me."

Cassie smiled up at the darkened ceiling, nuzzling closer against him. "This was incredible. I was in the middle of a saloon fight. I got to make love to you. I even thought I was being followed earlier tonight."

Hearing that made Clint's heart come to a complete stop.

"What did you say?"

THIRTEEN

Clint threw his clothes on while Cassie told him about what had happened after she'd left him with DelToro. He listened to what she had to say about the figure that had been following her and how that same figure had disappeared once she'd gotten around other people.

"I don't know why you're so worried," she said after she was done with her story. "It probably wasn't anything. I think I was still kind of nervous after being in the middle of that fight."

"You're probably right," Clint said while cinching his gun belt around his waist and fastening the buckle. "It was more than likely just some drunk."

But he didn't believe that. As much as he wanted to, he just couldn't get himself to go along with the notion that Cassie's fright was just a coincidence. Not after all he'd heard from DelToro about the killer that was out there gunning for him.

"Did you get a look at who might have been following you?" Clint asked.

Cassie, who hadn't even bothered getting dressed yet, leaned back against the headboard and took a moment to think. After a few contemplative breaths while tapping her chin thoughtfully, she shook her head. "Not really. All I saw was someone following me." She crawled forward to slip her hands over Clint's shoulders. "But it was nothing. Why don't you come back to bed?"

He could feel the growing urgency in her hands, as though the heat from her desire was emanating through her fingertips. Cassie's skin felt hot against him and he could feel her breath in his ear. In fact, as her hands slipped down his body and brushed against the modified Colt, her breaths sped up a bit.

"Did anyone see you come here?" Clint asked, doing his best to keep from being distracted.

She was getting frustrated now and turned him around to face her. "Nobody was following me. It was just someone staggering around in the dark and spooked me." As her hands began to pull apart his belt, she added, "I think it's so sweet of you to worry about me, though."

Taking hold of her wrists, Clint wanted to tell her that he had a very good reason to worry about her or anyone else that appeared to be close to him. He wanted to tell her that he was in the sights of a murderer and it would be best if he was there alone.

But he didn't tell her any of those things. That would have only frightened her. Instead, Clint kept his face calm and eased her hands off of him.

"I need to check on some things," he said.

"Things? What things? Why do you want to leave all of a sudden?"

"It's just some business I need to take care of." Still holding onto her wrists, Clint pulled her close to him once more so he could place a row of kisses along Cassie's neck. "How about you wait for me right here? You certain you weren't followed all the way to this room?"

She shook her head. "I wasn't. As soon as I got around someone else, that other person took off. I'm a grown woman, Clint. I can take care of myself you know. In fact, ever since I started spending time with you, I feel like I can take care of plenty."

"Good. I wouldn't mind taking care of you some more when I get back. Can you wait here for me?"

Cassie's eyes widened with excitement and she nodded.

Looking down at her naked body, Clint wanted nothing more than to put everything else aside and make good on his promise right then. But the nervousness in his belly wouldn't let him just yet. At least, he couldn't until he was certain that there wasn't someone watching the hotel or even that room at that very moment.

"I won't be gone for long," Clint said. "I promise."

Cassie planted a kiss on him that curled the toes within Clint's boots. When she moved away from him, she smiled at the look that was left on Clint's face.

"You'd better come back soon," she told him. "Or I might just find someone else to keep me happy."

Clint left her in the room and didn't walk down the hall until he heard the latch fall into place. Once he was certain that she was safe for the moment, he turned his thoughts to the man that was hunting him.

After hearing what DelToro and Cassie had to say, Clint didn't feel too paranoid thinking along those lines. He was being hunted. It wasn't the first time and it certainly wouldn't be the last, but that didn't make the situation any less serious.

What separated this from most other times when someone took it upon themselves to take a shot at him was that Clint couldn't recall Galloway's face. That thought alone made Clint even more uneasy as he made his way down the hall and out of the hotel.

Galloway could be any of the men he passed or none of them.

The killer could be lurking in any shadow and around any corner.

Rather than get swept up in the possibilities, Clint focused on the only things he knew for certain. Since he didn't have much by way of memories to go by, that left only what he could gather with his own senses. A hunter hoped that his prey would be foolish enough to become distracted enough to make a mistake. Fear was a weapon just as deadly as any blade or firearm, but only if it was allowed to take hold.

Clint was never much of one to be afraid.

It didn't suit him and he wasn't about to let its cold grip fit around him now.

Instead, he would do the one thing that removed all the power from a hunter's grasp. The hunted would become the hunter. At least that way Clint wasn't just wondering if DelToro's warnings had any merit. And if there was an axe hanging over Clint's head, looking for that axe was a hell of a lot better than just waiting for it to fall.

Clint stepped onto the boardwalk and took a look around at all the ground he needed to cover. He wasn't about to search the entire town for Galloway, but there were plenty of rooftops, alleyways and dark corners that could be used against him.

One thing was for certain; Clint was in for a long night.

FOURTEEN

It would have taken an inexperienced posse all night long to cover the area to Clint's satisfaction. Working on his own and using instincts and knowledge he'd acquired over the years, it took Clint a few hours to beat a path around the hotel that was wide enough to suit his needs. When he was finished, he knew for certain that Galloway had either been scared off or wasn't even around in the first place.

In fact, Clint was beginning to wonder if DelToro's information was even correct in the first place. By the time the first traces of daylight began to streak the eastern sky, Clint was dragging his feet back to the hotel where Cassie was waiting.

Throughout his search, Clint had picked out several unfamiliar faces, but none of them were those of a killer. Mostly, he'd seen old men shuffling along the boardwalk or women starting to make their daily rounds. Clint had tipped his hat to the locals and tried to return their chipper smiles, but he just didn't have much cheeriness left in him.

Clint stepped into the hotel, walked across the small lobby and up to the desk where a man in his late forties was preparing to make way for his replacement. As much as it pained him to do so, Clint pushed aside the tiredness that almost overtook him and put a smile onto his face.

"Getting ready to leave, huh?" Clint asked.

The clerk nodded and did his best to return Clint's smile. The effort was paltry at best, giving Clint an inkling of what he'd looked like to the early risers he'd passed on his way to the hotel.

"Amy should be here in a while," the clerk explained. "If it's breakfast you're after, then she's the one to talk to."

"Actually, I was hoping to meet up with a friend of mine. Did anyone come around here looking for me while I was gone? My name's Clint Adams."

After thinking it over for all of a second, the clerk shook his head. "Nope. No one came around looking for you."

"Maybe he just checked the register."

"A man, you say?"

Clint nodded.

"What's he look like?"

Hearing that question, Clint felt as though he'd sat down to the wrong game in a crowded poker hall. "Well, actually I don't know for certain. It's been a while and you know how people's faces change over the years."

Either the clerk bought what Clint was saying or he was in too much of a hurry to care. Either way, he shook his head one more time. "No, I don't think your friend's been around. I rented out a few rooms, but one was to a woman traveling on her own and the other was to a gentleman who didn't seem to be looking for anyone. In fact, he said he was waiting for his wife to arrive. That reminds me . . ."

The clerk let that sentence trail off as he picked up a pencil and scribbled a note onto the newspaper that sat folded upon the desk. Clint was able to make out the hastily written note as a simple reminder to Amy that the man in room number four was waiting for his wife.

"All right then," Clint said, feeling more tired by the

second. "I'll keep waiting in my room. Thanks for your help."

The clerk replied with a quick wave and came around from the other side of the desk the moment Clint headed down the hall. Before Clint even got to his room, he could hear the front door swinging open to let in an older woman who hummed to herself while the man stepped outside.

"Christ almighty," Clint said to himself under his breath. "I swear if DelToro's got me chasing my own tail I'll wring his neck."

After climbing the stairs, Clint's room was the third door down the hall. He could already feel himself settling under the sheets for some much-needed rest. His mood improved even more when he looked ahead a bit more to imagine how he and Cassie could spend the rest of the morning.

Clint reached out to put his hand on the door when something happened that made him forget about the fatigue that had such a firm hold on him. Not only was the door unlocked, but it also swung open easily the moment he bumped his fingers against the handle.

"Cassie?" Clint said without pushing the door open any further.

He didn't get so much as a single word in response.

In fact, as Clint leaned in close to the door, he couldn't hear anything coming from inside the room.

No movement.

No breathing.

Nothing.

As he slowly opened the door, Clint figured he would just find Cassie sleeping so soundly that she hadn't heard him come in. His hand remained over the holstered Colt, just in case he was wrong.

FIFTEEN

Clint pushed the door open in one fluid motion until the handle tapped against the wall.

"Cassie?" he said, shifting his eyes about the room to take in as much as he could.

As far as he could tell, the room didn't hold any unwanted surprises. Nobody was behind the door, standing against the walls or crouched in a corner. The curtains were drawn, so it was still a bit too dark for him to be sure but Clint didn't think anyone could be hiding without him noticing by now.

The only person he could see was Cassie, lying beneath the sheets with her head turned to one side. Clint walked around the bed and checked the rest of the room while he was at it. He'd already made her nervous enough before he'd left the last time, so he figured he might as well be relaxed before waking her this time.

"Don't worry, Cassie. It's just me."

Just to cover every possible angle, Clint dropped to one knee and took a quick look under the bed. When he found nothing but dust and a spider under there, he felt more than a little foolish. At least Cassie wasn't awake to see him acting like a kid checking for monsters.

62

Clint stood back up again, walked to the door, shut it and then made sure it was locked. He then turned his attention back to the bed where Cassie was laying and waiting for him. She looked peaceful laying there and had yet to stir since he'd gotten back.

The longer his eyes stayed on her, the more the tension that had been festering in the pit of his stomach grew to a rumbling boil.

Cassie wasn't moving.

Now that Clint was no longer walking and moving things around, he couldn't hear a single sound. The air was heavy with silence until it began to feel like a blanket tightening around his head.

"Cassie," Clint said insistently. "Wake up."

He reached over and put a hand on her shoulder to shake her, freezing in place the moment his hand made contact with her skin.

She was still warm but only from the sun that managed to slip past the fabric of the curtains and fall upon her body. Beneath the flesh, there should have been the warmth that every living creature had. It should have been there, but it wasn't in Cassie.

Not anymore.

"Oh Jesus," Clint said as he dropped down to get closer to her face. "What the hell happened to you?"

He took hold of her by the shoulder and rolled her so she was laying flat on her back. Clint's motions were urgent, yet still gentle, as though part of him thought that he might harm her if he didn't take care. When she was on her back, her head lolled against the pillow like a broken doll's. The sight brought a low, angry growl to the back of Clint's throat.

"Son of a bitch!"

The noise he made was part curse and part animal reaction. Clint's fist slammed against the headboard, knocking so powerfully against the wall that it left a deep crack in the wood. Before he reached down to move the hair from her face, Clint forced his fist to open and took deliberate care to be gentle with her.

Part of him didn't even want to see the blood that had seeped into the mattress beneath her. That part wanted to just turn back the clock and stay by her side rather than leave her alone in the room. But it was too late for any of that. Once that realization set in, Clint pulled in a deep breath and took a look at the gruesome picture in front of him.

Cassie was still naked beneath the sheets. A deep gash had been opened in her side that started in the middle of her torso and went all the way around to her spine. The cut traced a line between two of her ribs and had drained most of her blood into the sheets and mattress beneath her.

Although Clint was no doctor, he could tell that Cassie must have either been caught by surprise or was made to trust whoever had wound up killing her. The expression on her face was still peaceful, even serene. Apart from the slash across her side and back, there wasn't even so much as a bruise to mar her skin.

Rather than pull the curtains back, he went over to the room's single lantern and twisted the knob. When the flame rose up from the wick, Clint was able to see even more of what was left of Cassie. The bed was a rumpled mess, but that was how he'd left it. Nothing in the room was disturbed and every bit of furniture was in its place.

With more light to go by, Clint was able to see some redness in her face that hadn't been there before. That's when he noticed the pillow laying next to her head looked as though it had been clenched in someone's hand. Sure enough, when he picked up the pillow and turned it over, he could see streaks of moisture staining the material.

That moisture could have been saliva, but there was no mistaking the blood smeared into the linen as well. Almost reverently, Clint set the pillow down and took another look at Cassie.

The sight of her made Clint's stomach clench with an equal mix of anger at what had happened and regret for not staying with her the entire time. With those regrets weighing down on him, he examined her one last time to see if there was anything he'd missed.

The single wound was as precise as it was fatal. It reminded Clint of a surgical cut, splitting open the flesh in a clean line to empty her blood into the mattress.

Just then, as his eyes moved over her body in search of anything else that might help him figure out what had happened, Clint spotted something that had almost gotten past him. Kneeling beside the bed, Clint reached out to take hold of Cassie's hand.

Her skin was so much colder than when he'd left her. It was even colder than when he'd touched her only moments ago. Hers wasn't the first dead body he'd ever seen, but it was still difficult to get past just how hollow that corpse felt.

Setting aside his growing rage as best he could, Clint took hold of Cassie's right arm by the wrist. The sheet draped over that arm was clean except for a subtle crimson taint. It was that stain that had caught his attention and now that he got a closer look at it, he could tell that the blood hadn't quite soaked all the way through the cotton.

Pulling aside the sheet, Clint saw that he was right. There was blood on the sheet but not nearly as much as what had soaked into the mattress. The blood came from her right hand.

Specifically, it came from her right index finger.

Even more specifically, it came from the nub which was all that was left of her right index finger.

Clint couldn't take it any longer.

He got up and pulled the sheet over Cassie's body before walking out of the room. The moment he stepped into the hall, he thought back to what he'd heard from the desk clerk about who'd come and gone from the hotel while he was away.

His eyes shifted toward the door beside his own, recalling that the clerk had mentioned a man and woman were the ones to rent it out. With his hand lowering toward the Colt at his side, Clint walked to that door, lifted his foot and slammed his boot just below the door's handle.

The Colt was drawn and his sights were set upon the man waiting inside the room even before the door could smack against the wall.

"Good lord!" the man sitting in bed shouted while floundering beneath the sheets as if he wasn't sure where to go.

"Stay right where you are," Clint warned. Looking at the woman in bed with the man, he said, "You too. Just stay put and do as I say."

"Please don't hurt us," the man whimpered. "We don't have much money, but whatever we have is yours. Just take it and leave."

The woman was on the verge of tears but was too frightened to let them flow. Her face was frozen in terror, right along with the rest of her.

"Your hands," Clint said. "Let's see them. Both of you."

The couple raised their hands and held them over their heads.

"No," Clint said. "Palms up."

Exchanging confused glances, the couple lowered their arms and extended them out in front of them with their palms up. Although they were trembling uncontrollably, they held their hands out as they were told while Clint looked them over.

When he was done examining their hands, Clint looked around the room. "Stay right there," he said to the couple. "I just want to see your clothes."

Clint was finished just as footsteps rushed up from the hallway. There were confused, panicked voices, but Clint didn't hear any of them. All he did was holster the Colt and look toward the person that seemed to be in charge.

"What's going on here?" an older woman demanded. "I've sent for the marshal."

"Good," Clint said as he stepped past her. "I'll be down the hall."

SIXTEEN

It wasn't long before every man wearing a badge was at Clint's hotel. To Clint, on the other hand, it seemed to have taken days for the lawmen to arrive. All the while, he'd been busy on his own while ignoring all the questions that kept coming his way.

It wasn't so much that he couldn't hear the people speaking to him or didn't want to answer. He just felt like he was moving through a dream. As he carried out his tasks, Clint was thinking about Cassie and how he could still smell her on his hands.

Her voice still rang in his ears, and if he stopped to think about it long enough, he could even feel the lingering traces of her warmth on his hands. Since the last warmth he'd felt of her was from her blood, Clint was doing his best to put those thoughts from his mind as well as putting some distance between himself and what had happened.

After a while, Clint found himself standing in the room just behind the hotel's small lobby. There was a little rolltop desk and a few chairs there as well as some simple paintings hanging on the wall. Looking around, Clint felt almost as if his mind had just caught up with the rest of him.

The first face to catch Clint's eye was DelToro's. Standing next to the Mexican was another large man wearing a badge. The badge was different from DelToro's, but they both looked at him with the same expressions on their faces.

Considering what had happened, Clint couldn't say he blamed them for looking at him that way.

"How you feeling, amigo?" DelToro asked.

Clint nodded and took a breath. "Tired."

The man beside DelToro nodded. "I'll bet you are. By the sound of it, you've been pretty busy." Seeing the questioning expression upon Clint's face, the other lawman introduced himself. "I'm Bill Lockley. Marshal Lockley, actually."

Once again noting the differences in the two men's badges, Clint said, "You'd be the town law?"

Lockley nodded once. "I sure would. And you'd be Clint Adams. Although we haven't met quite yet, I sure have heard plenty about you."

Clint's eyes had already shifted back to DelToro. "Did you get a look at Cassie?"

DelToro nodded. Before he could say anything, however, Lockley stepped in.

"We saw the girl and we saw plenty of others that're in this hotel," the local lawman said. "Some of the things we're hearing don't make you sound all too good."

Clint moved his eyes to look back at Lockley. When he did, there was enough of a fire in them to shut the lawman up for a second. Fortunately, that was all the time Clint needed to ask, "Do you think I killed her?"

"Not at all," DelToro replied before Lockley could say anything to make matters worse. "I know you couldn't have done such a thing."

"Well he may be convinced," Lockley grunted. "But I sure ain't. I've got witnesses here saying that you busted in on them like a man possessed, waving a gun around and putting good folks in fear for their lives. That may be just fine for the *Federales*, but it don't sit well with me at all."

Clint shook his head and took a moment to think, not wanting to spit out something that would only cast him in an even worse light. Before he could say anything, DelToro once again stepped up.

"Don't worry about Adams, Bill. I'm telling you that he couldn't have done this."

"Wait a second," Clint said, his eyes now shifting to regard DelToro a bit differently than before. "How are you so sure about that?"

The Mexican paused but knew that it was no use to wait much longer before saying, "I've got some men looking out for you."

"Looking out for me or watching me?"

"Whichever way you want to cut it, they would have known if you did something like this." DelToro fixed his eyes on Lockley and added, "Clint didn't kill that girl."

Although the local lawman seemed somewhat pacified by what DelToro had said, he began to pace about the room with his hands flailing at his sides. "All right. Adams didn't kill her, so who did? I don't suppose these men of yours know that, do they?"

"Galloway did it," Clint said. "He did it to send me a message."

DelToro's head snapped as he looked at Clint straight on. "What message?"

"Just a little reminder to make sure I knew it was him that was after me. He took her finger." Clint paused as the grisly memory flashed through his mind with all too much clarity. "He took her trigger finger."

SEVENTEEN

Lockley looked from one man to the other with growing frustration. "For all we know, that was just some coincidence. Maybe the killer was after a ring or something."

"She wasn't wearing a ring," Clint said, getting to his feet. "She was cut open and left so I could find her. Nothing was taken from the room and nothing was left behind. Cassie was a seamstress who liked to kick her heels up every so often. That doesn't exactly make a person mortal enemies with someone who would do something like this."

"Then maybe she was killed by some animal who just likes to kill. That's been known to happen, you know."

"I know, Lockley," Clint replied. "And it's not your concern anymore."

The local marshal's face become red with anger, but Clint didn't much care about that. Instead, he turned to DelToro who was looking at him expectantly. "How long have you been keeping watch on me?"

But Lockley wasn't about to be shunted aside so easily. The local lawman dropped his thick hand upon Clint's shoulder and turned him around to face him. The anger in Lockley's eyes was matched only by the fire in Clint's.

"I've cut you plenty of slack, Adams," Lockley fumed.

"But this is still my town and I won't stand for being pushed around by a couple the likes of you and Mister U.S. Marshal here. I've still got a killer to find."

"So do I," Clint replied.

"Then since you say you didn't do it, I need to find out who did."

Clint felt like he was waking up from a bad dream. Although he'd been content to sit still and catch his breath for a moment, all he wanted now was to get out of that room. "Look, Marshal, we're wasting time. We need to get after Galloway."

"And what makes you think he hasn't ridden out of town already? Lord knows he's had plenty of time!"

"Because he's after me," Clint answered plainly. "Murdering Cassie was a way to get to me. Otherwise, she wouldn't have been laying there on display and nobody would have taken the time to cut her finger off."

"Then what about the others in the hotel?" Lockley asked as he pushed Clint aside and started walking for the door. "You stay here and I'll check on them."

"I already checked," Clint said. "They didn't kill her either."

Fixing his eyes on Clint, Lockley appeared to be one second away from laughing at him. "Is that a fact? Well you're a regular detective, ain't you?"

"Cassie was cut open and bled to death," Clint explained. "Whoever killed her would have had blood on their hands or clothes. I checked out everything belonging to the other guests and didn't find a drop of blood."

"Is that what you were doing kicking down doors?"

"Actually, yes."

"Then maybe they burned the clothes or tossed them out the window."

"Did your men check for a fire or anything in the street below the windows?"

Lockley stopped for a moment. The expression on his

face made it plain to see that he didn't like what he was about to say. "Yeah. I had someone look. They didn't find anything."

Although Clint had a few choice words ready for the local marshal, he had to give the man credit for speaking the truth. Rather than stir up anything else, Clint looked over to DelToro and said, "You know Galloway did this."

Lockley was waiting for the answer to that question as well.

DelToro nodded without hesitation. "Yes."

"Jesus Christ," Lockley grunted. "I've got a couple real experts here. If you knew so much," he said to DelToro, "then why didn't you step in before that poor girl got herself cut up?"

"This is something Galloway would do," the Mexican replied. "But trying to guess what he'll do beforehand is like trying to predict which way the wind will blow."

Tossing his hands in the air out of sheer frustration, Lockley said, "Oh, that's just great. Just goddamn perfect!"

But while the local marshal fumed, Clint and DelToro squared off with a quiet determination.

Once again, Clint asked, "How long have you been watching me?"

"Just since you got to town," DelToro said. "Before that, we didn't even know where you were or how to get in touch with you."

"So this works out just perfectly, doesn't it?"

"No, Adams. This is a terrible night. This is also why I wanted to use any means necessary to put this animal down. I told you his killing has been reckless and this proves my point. This is also messier than Galloway normally works and it's not the sort of target he usually goes after.

"Like you said, he's after you. Plain and simple. I only wish you had been there when he stepped foot in this room. Maybe then you could have done this world a big favor by taking Galloway out of it."

Now that his heart was beating at its normal rate and his blood wasn't pounding through his veins like a flood, Clint found he could think a hell of a lot clearer. At that moment, he was thinking about the expression on Cassie's face and the condition of the room.

"He wouldn't have showed himself if I'd have been there," Clint said in a way that was kind of a revelation to himself as well as to the others in the room.

"How do you know that?" Lockley asked.

"It's an instinct, but I just know it's true. He knew what he was doing. He didn't just kick down the door and slaughter her. He got up close, won her confidence and then executed her." Although they were true, those words left a bitter taste in Clint's mouth.

DelToro's face was grim as he nodded slowly. "That sounds like the way he works."

"And speaking of work," Clint said, "are you still looking for someone to track Galloway down?"

"I sure am. Besides the fee, I'll give you some money for expenses and—"

"Keep your money," Clint interrupted. "This isn't about the fee. And keep your men from following me. They'll only get in the way."

EIGHTEEN

The sun was blazing down upon Brigham Way as though the town was being punished for what had happened during the night. Heat roiled through the air and sunk into anything that got in its way, causing flesh to burn and waves to ripple up off the ground.

Although news had spread about the grisly death of Cassie Dawson, the locals did their best to go about their business without dwelling on the morbid details. There would be plenty of time for gossip once things had gotten somewhat back to normal. For the time being, the busybodies were too scared to spread bloody rumors.

The streets had been all but emptied on account of the heat as well as the previous night's killing. It was one thing for a man to get shot because of an insult he'd made or a wrong he'd committed. It was even something else for someone to die in the midst of a fight. To that end, the scuffle in the Red Rooster was already being joked about.

But what had happened to Cassie was something else entirely and everyone felt it. If she had been killed for any obvious reason, even a foolish one, the crime wouldn't have seemed so atrocious. But Cassie had been cut open and bled out as if she'd fallen prey to a demon in the night.

Things like that shook a town. They shook it right down to the core and Brigham Way was no exception. Cassie's death left the streets quiet and empty except for the newly deputized men who now patrolled them with shotguns resting in the crooks of their arms.

The locals weren't the only ones to feel the effects. Clint was still going over in his mind what had happened, trying to think of what he could have done though he knew there was nothing that would have helped.

He was in the livery saddling Eclipse when Clint heard someone walking through the dried hay strewn over the floor. DelToro wore a fresh set of clothes but still looked as though he hadn't slept in a week.

"I appreciate this, Adams," the Mexican said. "I know that doesn't make things any better, but there really wasn't anything you could have done to save her."

Clint smirked, but the gesture was without any trace of humor. "Has Galloway done this before, or is reading minds a new requirement for the U.S. marshals?"

"Neither. You look troubled and it doesn't take more than one guess to figure out why." When Clint didn't say anything to that, DelToro walked up and leaned against the stall next to Eclipse's. "I didn't know she was that important to you. Did you know her for long?"

"We'd met some time ago when I was in town before. She was a good woman who liked to spend time with the wrong sort of man."

"And what sort is that?"

"The sort that gets her killed," Clint said as though he was spitting out the rotten words. When he cinched up the last buckle of the saddle, he pulled it into place hard enough to get Eclipse to shift uneasily in place. Clint reached out to soothe the Darley Arabian with a few pats on the neck.

"I got a closer look at the woman and the room. Even if

you were there at the time, it wouldn't have changed things," DelToro said.

Clint nodded. "Yeah. I know. She was murdered very deliberately. Nothing was knocked over. Hell, she looked like she was sleeping when I found her. Galloway didn't kick the door off its hinges. He took his time with her and did what he wanted to do, knowing that I would find her like that."

"And if you stayed with her all night long," DelToro added, "he would have just waited for you to go to the outhouse or get a drink of water and the result would have been the same." Pulling in a deep breath, he spoke in a more natural tone. "I hope you're not going to go after him angry, señor. That's what Galloway wants."

"I know."

"And since she was just an acquaintance, you should just—"

"Don't tell me to forget about her, DelToro," Clint interrupted. "She might not have been family or my wife, but I won't just forget about what happened that easily. We might have just shared a bed for a night or two, but I can't abide to let what happened to her slide. I won't even try to play it down.

"There are no little deaths," Clint added. "Sometimes, after all the killing I've seen, it's too easy to forget about that. There's plenty of blood that gets spilled for no good reason, but most of it happens to men who live a life where such things are common.

"Cassie was a seamstress. She didn't live a dangerous life and she didn't deserve what happened. Not by a long shot."

DelToro listened to every word and by the time Clint was finished, the marshal had his hat in hand and his head bowed. Nodding, he said, "I didn't mean to step out of line."

"You didn't. This whole thing just touches a nerve."

"And it should. You wouldn't be much of a man if it didn't. That's why I was certain you would help me."

Finishing up the last bit of preparation for getting Eclipse ready to ride and his saddlebags in place, Clint opened the gate to Eclipse's stall and climbed onto the stallion's back. "I said I'd help and I meant it. But I also meant what I said about your men. Whoever you've got following me, call them off. I won't be too happy if I find out I've still got a shadow after so many fair warnings."

"I understand."

"I'll also need to know everything I can about Galloway. Where he goes, where he's been, who he talks to, all of it. I assume you've got that for me already."

DelToro reached into the inner pocket of his vest and pulled out a bundle of papers held together by a length of twine. "Here you go."

Clint took the papers and tucked them into his own pocket. "All right then. Where will you be if I need to get in touch with you?"

"I'm staying here. After what happened, I doubt Lockley would let me go before chewing me out for at least another day or two."

"Good. When I find something, I'll send word."

"Where will you start, señor? Galloway could be anywhere."

"I'm the one he's after," Clint said while flicking the reins and getting Eclipse to head for the stable's door. "So you just let me worry about it from here."

NINETEEN

Galloway was in unfriendly territory. Then again, for a man on the run from as many people as he was, just about any place besides a few choice caves were unfriendly to some degree or other. That kind of life tested a man to show what he was truly made of and if he was cut out to lead the life of an outlaw.

Some men cracked under the pressure of being hunted, while others ran away the first chance they got. Galloway fell into another category, however. He fell into the category of those who tested themselves and passed with flying colors.

He thrived on the chase, whether he was predator or prey. He saw every hunt as a challenge and the kill was his reward. If he had to take a bullet every so often himself, then so be it. Passing that test meant knowing that death was always a heartbeat away.

At the moment, Galloway's heartbeat was a quick thump in his chest. Of course, nobody would know that by looking at him. On the outside, he was calm and collected, just another stranger riding slowly down the streets of Brigham Way.

He held the reins loosely in one hand while keeping the

other on his knee where it wasn't too far from the holster under the flap of his jacket. The sun was beating down mercilessly, making it feel like his clothes were melting to his skin. Still, Galloway maintained his easygoing mannerisms, even tipping his hat to the ladies he passed and waving casually to folks he saw on either side of the street.

All the while, his eyes were shifting back and forth, studying each person carefully. He was on the lookout for the same things as always: badges, guns, stares that were trained too long in his direction. Apart from those things, he was also looking for something very specific.

He was looking for Clint Adams. In fact, he'd been doing that for a long time.

Now, just like every other time when that man's name drifted through Galloway's mind, he couldn't help but think back to what had started this particular hunt in the first place . . .

It had been a little over a year ago and Galloway had been in the process of making a name for himself. To rise in the ranks of the professional killer, a man's name and reputation were everything. He couldn't just create his reputation and it wasn't enough to just put in enough time or shoot enough men.

A reputation that was worth anything at all had to be earned. Galloway had been working toward that goal for a few months and had already made quite a bit of progress. He'd picked fights that would later become saloon legends. He'd humiliated other men who thought they were bad and had done so in front of an audience.

More than that, he'd tracked down men who'd rightfully earned their own reputations and gunned them down like dogs in the street. After putting six holes through a feared gunfighter in Abilene, Galloway was approached by a broker from Nevada who specialized in fixing messy problems for very rich men.

"I need someone killed," the broker told Galloway after arranging a meeting in a small desert town called Las Rias.

Galloway was well into his twenties, but looking back on that day, he seemed to himself like such a kid. At the time, he'd nodded coolly and acted as though these weren't the very words he'd been hoping to hear from a man like this broker.

"I can help you out," Galloway replied.

The broker smirked a bit and fixed his gaze a little harder on the young man in front of him. "Don't you even want to know who it is?"

Shrugging, Galloway said, "If you want to tell me."

For a moment, the broker looked like he was about to laugh. Galloway thought he'd said or done something wrong that might just cost him the career he was after. But then the broker settled back into his chair and rubbed his chin thoughtfully.

"How many men have you killed?"

Galloway's first reaction was always to lie. The only other question that was more likely to get an untrue response was how many women a man's bedded. But this wasn't just some saloon and the broker wasn't just some man looking to swap bawdy stories.

This was a professional meeting and Galloway figured he should act accordingly.

"Seven," Galloway replied. "I shot more than that, but I know for certain that seven are dead."

"How do you know?"

"Because I made sure of it myself."

The broker waited for a moment and then nodded. "You know something? I believe you. Most young punks like you would go into every bloody detail or wouldn't have mentioned any total number that wasn't at least in the double digits.

"I knew a whore once who told me that the more a man talks, the less he's done." Nodding again, the broker said, "I can believe you've filled seven graves."

"Is that enough?" Galloway asked.

"What do you mean?"

"For the job. Is that enough to qualify me for this job you had in mind?"

The men were sitting in a small cantina. Looking back on that day, Galloway remembered that fact only because the broker had leaned back in his chair to let the waitress take their glasses and refill them. Strangely enough, waiting for that waitress to do her business was almost unbearable for the younger Galloway.

Finally, the broker leaned forward again and lifted the glass to his mouth. "Being a killer isn't like being a carpenter or mason." He sipped from his glass and set it down as though he was discussing the weather. "It's something that a man is born with. If you'd never killed anyone, then I would have already left by now. Even one or two kills is enough to tell what you've got inside."

"Yeah?"

"Yes. You take two men and set them against each other. One is tough as nails and can punch through a goddamn brick wall and the other is a killer. Which is going to win?"

"In a fistfight or a gunfight?"

The broker smiled, placed his hand flat upon the table and leaned forward so he could stare directly into Galloway's eyes. "It doesn't matter. A killer will always win because he's not worried about the rules or what kind of fight it is or what the other man's strengths may be. A killer focuses on his target's weaknesses and always makes sure that he doesn't get into a fight unless it's one he can win.

"Killing for money isn't about winning, losing or looking good for the ladies. It's about killing. That's it. Pure and simple. I think you already know that. Or, at least you know it on some level. That's why I'm going to give you a chance."

Galloway's eyes widened as though a twelve-ounce T-bone had been set in front of him after a month of eating stale bread. "That's great. I really appreciate this and I know I can do plenty of good work for you."

"We'll see if you're still so anxious when you find out who you'll be after."

TWENTY

It had happened right after dinner.

Three days after Galloway's meeting with the broker, he found himself one town over living in a room that was barely fit for a rat. He had his first real job as a professional killer and felt as if he was sitting on top of the world.

He'd been watching his target for a day and a half and picked this as the night when he would make his move. He didn't even know the man's name. All he knew was that he was one of the most dangerous men in the county and had stirred up enough shit to get a damn good price put out for his scalp.

Galloway was nervous as hell, even though he'd spilled plenty of blood before that night. This wasn't like those other times. He wasn't out to make a name for himself. He'd already caught the right person's attention and now it was time to prove that he was worthy of it. Unlike those other times, he had a hell of a lot more to lose.

From what he'd gathered about the man he was after, Galloway was also fairly certain the odds weren't anywhere close to being in his favor. But it was too late to worry about that. Turning back now would mean throwing out everything he'd been working for up to then.

It was a cool night, but Galloway was still sweating. He checked his pistol one more time to make sure he was loaded. He also checked the other gun he was carrying to make sure that wouldn't fail him either. Once the cylinders were snapped back into place and he'd taken a deep breath, it was time to get to work.

Right on schedule, the man Galloway was after walked out into the open and into the street. Galloway's hands lowered to his holstered guns as he walked straight out to meet him.

The target wasn't the sort to be caught off his guard and spotted Galloway immediately. His eyes narrowed and he started to ask a question, but stopped himself when he realized that Galloway wasn't exactly in the talking mood.

The other man's hand went for his gun, but Galloway had already drawn his and was taking aim. A shot blasted through the air, followed by the sound of lead slapping against flesh.

Everything at that moment went deathly quiet.

People walking by on the street froze, not wanting to believe what they'd just seen.

Rather than take a moment to let it all sink in for himself, Galloway was firing another shot into the man. His first bullet had drilled a messy hole through the target's stomach and the second made it a little higher into his chest.

That second shot stopped the man in his tracks, his hand still trying to pull his gun from its holster.

Galloway stepped up until he was directly in front of the man. Standing less than a foot or two away, he looked straight into the target's eyes and started lifting his gun.

The other man was still on his feet and trying to pull in another breath. A wet sucking sound came from his chest and blood drizzled onto the ground in a steady stream. His breath and clothes stank of the opium den he'd been leaving when Galloway had found him.

The spot for that meeting was no coincidence. After Galloway had learned that his target frequented the place in the Chinese section of Las Rias, he knew that would be the perfect place to confront him. The fact that the other man was there so often meant that he wouldn't be in any condition to fight when he came out.

Before meeting with the broker, Galloway would have thought that picking that time for that reason was beneath him. But it wasn't a fight that Galloway was after.

It was death.

And death was exactly what he'd gotten.

The target was still so dizzy from the opium he'd smoked that he barely seemed to realize that he'd been shot. All he knew for certain was that he was having a hard time moving and was starting to fall over. It could have been from the drug or from the pains that now started to burn in his stomach and chest.

The other man was still trying to lift his gun, but that was merely a reflex. It was too late for him now. All that was left was for Galloway to step up and finish the job.

And that was exactly what he did.

Galloway slapped the gun from his target's hand and kicked him in the lower part of his gut to drop him onto the ground. From there, he pressed the barrel of his pistol against the other man's forehead and pulled his trigger.

Folks in Las Rias would talk about that day for years as one of the most cold-blooded, gruesome things they'd ever seen.

Galloway thought of it as the beginning of a promising career.

TWENTY-ONE

"I knew you had it in you kid," the broker had said while handing over Galloway's money.

Even though the envelope he was given was thick with bills, Galloway hardly even noticed. "You think I did a good job?"

"A good job? That was public and messy, just what the client wanted. It'll be a long time before anyone pulls what that poor bastard tried to do. And you didn't even take a scratch for yourself. I've got to admit that you did even better than I'd hoped."

"Great. When's my next job?"

"You're a little eager, huh? Well, that's understandable considering the circumstances. Still, you should probably lay low for a bit. There's likely to be men after you."

"If you're talking about the law, don't even bother. I shook them off my tail after less than a day's ride."

"Still, I don't want to be too hasty. You've become a valuable commodity."

Galloway liked the sound of that and couldn't help but sit up a little straighter when he heard the admiration in the broker's voice.

"There's a bonus in that envelope," the broker said.

"Just a bit to hold you over for supplies, travel expenses and such until things cool off. Never let it be said that I didn't take care of my workers."

"So I'm one of your regular employees?"

"After what you did in Las Rias, I wouldn't have it any other way."

It took a couple more weeks before Galloway heard from the broker again. That time was spent living close to the vest while one posse after another was formed to hunt him down. Apparently, the man he'd killed in Las Rias was a little more important than Galloway had thought.

But none of that bothered him too much. What was important was that he was living the life he wanted and with the money he'd earned after that first job, the future looked awfully bright.

Galloway sent telegrams that were never answered to a contact that supposedly led to the broker. Just when he was starting to wonder if his career was actually a one-time job, Galloway got a reply from one of those telegrams.

It hadn't been that long, but Galloway was like a kid waiting for Christmas morning. He took the first train into Carson City and met up with the broker at a little café that was patterned after an English tea shop. The European touches were lost on Galloway. He was only interested in one thing.

"When's my next job?" he asked anxiously.

The broker patted the air to calm him down. "No need to get jumpy. Didn't I give you enough money to buy yourself a woman to take some of that edge off?"

"I just want to work again."

"Well, there hasn't been a whole lot coming my way in that respect."

"Then why'd you have me meet you here?"

It was hard to say whether the broker was annoyed or impressed by Galloway's eagerness. Looking back on it, Galloway figured it was more the latter.

"There is one job," the broker said, "but it may be too

much for you. Then again, it might just be the one to make you a known man throughout the whole country."

"Where is it?"

"Don't you want to know who it is?"

Galloway smirked, thinking back to their first conversation. Jesus, it seemed like that was an entire lifetime ago. "Only if you want to tell me."

"This time, I think I should."

"All right," Galloway said, sensing the seriousness in the broker's tone. "Go ahead."

"His name's Clint Adams. You ever hear of him?"

"The Gunsmith? Hell yes, I've heard of him. Who hasn't?"

"Seems he's run afoul of some important people who are willing to pay handsomely to have him taken out."

"And you want me to do it?"

"Do you think you can?"

Although Galloway's first impulse was to accept the job no matter what, he took a minute to seriously consider this one. It was one thing to build a reputation and eventually a career. It was another thing entirely to sign up for a job that was something close to suicide.

"Who wants Adams dead?" Galloway asked.

"That don't concern you. All that matters is that whoever it is decided to hire on a professional gun hand from outside his own people. That's where I come in and that can also be where you come in.

"You can say no to this and I won't think any less of you. But if you say yes, you know who you'll be going up against. I've heard plenty of things about Clint Adams and not all of them could possibly be true. Still, he's hell and Jesus with a pistol. That much is certain. If you take him down, I don't have to tell you what that would mean for the both of us."

The broker gave him a moment to consider the possibilities.

"You'll be known as the man who killed a legend," the broker said. "With that under your belt, I can hire you out on some jobs that are so big you'll only have to do one or two a year to live like a king. We can name our price and men will pay it. Think about that."

Galloway was thinking about it all right.

He could imagine the glory of gunning down someone like The Gunsmith. He could also imagine how someone like Clint Adams had become known as such a lethal man.

Galloway knew all too well what it took to build a reputation into a legend. There was no way to luck into something like that. Clint Adams had to be fast and he had to be deadly. Otherwise, he would have been dead meat on a platter.

Going up against someone like that could bring death quicker than he could imagine. In fact, Galloway had heard about Adams killing men so fast they didn't even hear the gunshot before they were stretched out on the ground.

With all that in mind, Galloway could think of only three words to say to the broker.

"Where is he?"

TWENTY-TWO

It turned out that Clint Adams was in a town called Wescott, Nevada. Galloway didn't know why Adams was there or who he'd pissed off, but none of that mattered to a true professional. Even though he'd only had a little bit of experience, Galloway consider himself to be a true professional. If he wasn't, the broker never would have bothered with him.

If he wasn't, he wouldn't have made it this far, with so much in his bank account, and still be alive to enjoy it.

Looking back on it, even Galloway had to admit he'd been a little overzealous. At the time, however, he was riding high and nobody could stop him. The rest of the world was made up of people that were either victims or clients.

Simple and easy.

The way things turned out, it was actually neither.

Adams wasn't hard to find. Once he got to Wescott, all Galloway had to do was keep his ears open to get an idea of where to start looking. That part had taken up the first ten minutes of his visit, and the next day was spent in getting a look at the legend for himself.

To Galloway, Adams was just a man. He was friendly enough and walked with a definite confidence about him, but he was a man all the same. What got under Galloway's skin most of all was the way everyone else seemed to cater to Adams.

He would have understood if the locals were afraid of him or if they were trying to stay on Adams's good side. Galloway might have even understood if they were after a favor from the gunman, but it didn't appear as though any of those things were true. Folks just tended to be drawn to Adams and that went double for the ladies.

In the end, though, all of that was just a side thought for Galloway. He was more concerned with tracing Adams's steps and picking out a spot that would place him a few paces ahead of The Gunsmith once the moment of truth finally arrived.

Galloway spoke to a few of the gun hands working for the client and got just enough out of the conversation to arrange something of a trap for Adams. That was a difficult decision to make, but Galloway knew it was the best possible choice.

Anyone out to make a name for themselves could have challenged Adams at any time. There were plenty of opportunities while Adams was going for his meals or even playing cards, but Galloway wasn't out to prove anything to anybody.

He was out to do his job.

Just like a true professional.

When the time came, Galloway made sure he'd picked his spot and planned out exactly what he would do. He couldn't allow himself to think about who he was going after or what would happen once the job was done. There would be plenty of time to savor the kill later. And after that, glory.

The spot Galloway had chosen was at the mouth of an alley across the street from where Adams was going to be. He knew Adams would be there because Galloway had taken the time to arrange for him to be herded there by the client's gun hands. The local thugs were only too eager to cooperate since Adams had proven to be a pain in their collective ass.

Looking back on that night, Galloway found it to be a blur of images and emotions. He'd been standing in the darkness with gun in hand. His eyes had been focused upon the same spot for so long that they were starting to burn in their sockets. The headache that followed soon faded into a haze that must have been something close to the touch of opium felt by his previous target.

He was excited to be on the verge of such a major change in his life and also nervous to be throwing down against one of the most feared and respected gunmen in the world. Galloway pushed that straight out of his mind and focused on one thing only: the kill.

Before too long, he could hear a commotion in the distance as the fight between Adams and the other gunmen got under way. Galloway wasn't sure how that fight was going and didn't care. All that mattered was that Adams was brought into his sights.

And then it happened.

Adams came into view, holding off a handful of men who were all shooting at him like they were fighting a war. Watching from a distance, it was hard for Galloway to tell who was herding who. Even with all the lead flying through the air, Adams was calm and collected.

The Gunsmith earned his name and every bit of his reputation in Galloway's eyes. He fired back with expert precision at the gunmen chasing him. He fought back the tide of gunfire and made it look easy in the process.

He stood amidst the bullet-laden air and held his ground. It was like watching a man stand in the middle of a rainstorm without getting wet. Not only did Adams not get hit, but he also placed his own bullets perfectly so he could pick off his attackers one by one.

Galloway lifted his weapon and sighted down the barrel.

He shook his head when he got a better look at the other gunmen who were pulling their triggers as fast as they could without even looking. Their arms flailed about wildly, making it seem like a miracle that they weren't shooting themselves in the process.

A smile had crept onto Galloway's face as he waited for the moment to take his shot. Adams may have been doing just fine against the hired punks, but he was about to be dropped by a true professional. In fact, he wouldn't even see it coming.

Suddenly, Adams spun around to get a look at where he was going. His eyes took in the street and surrounding storefronts, soaking it all up in a matter of a second. His eyes were drawn straight to Galloway as though he could somehow hear the blood rushing through the killer's veins.

Galloway kept his calm even as he saw Adams turn to shift his aim in his direction. There was no way for the man to turn and fire with any amount of accuracy, especially since Galloway already had his gun up and ready to fire.

But no matter how much he'd heard about Adams or how much he'd imagined about The Gunsmith, there was no way in hell Galloway could know just how fast Adams truly was.

One moment, Galloway was lining up a shot.

The next moment, Adams was looking.

Galloway had been spotted.

Adams turned.

Adams fired.

It happened so quickly that Galloway felt as though he'd been frozen in place. He was still thinking about pulling his trigger when he found himself staggering backward and sucking in a quick, painful breath.

After that breath, he realized that the gun he'd been holding was now laying on the ground. Galloway didn't remember dropping the weapon, which got him to look down at the hand that had been holding it.

Blood was spraying from that hand, more precisely, from the tip of what used to be his trigger finger.

That's when the pain really kicked in.

TWENTY-THREE

It was a few days before Galloway was able to head back into Carson City. The broker was supposed to be meeting him to discuss what happened with the assignment. Even though he knew things couldn't have gone worse, Galloway still had some hope of salvaging the situation.

Without that hope, Galloway figured he might as well have been killed back in that dark alley.

They met in the same tea shop as before. This time, the smell of the leaves and the scent of candles burning were no comfort to Galloway. He sat at the table and ignored the dainty cup that was set before him. Finally, he spotted the broker walking in through the front door.

"Good to see you," the broker said as he took a seat and calmly motioned for the waitress. "I hear things didn't quite go according to plan."

Galloway started to talk but stopped when the waitress came by to take the other man's order. She smiled at both of them and quickly returned with a cup of steaming tea.

"Not according to plan?" Galloway said. "You could say that."

The broker sipped his tea and said, "I could also say the

job was fucked up six different ways to Sunday, but that wouldn't be so polite. What happened?"

Galloway gave him the short version of the story. He outlined his plan, the things he'd done to set it up and all the pains he'd taken to see it through. Still, even though he glossed over some of the details, he couldn't help but be disappointed in himself when he described what had happened once Adams was in his sights.

Judging by the look on the broker's face, "disappointed" wasn't quite strong enough of a word.

"You know who Adams is, right?" the broker asked. "I thought we went all through this."

"We did. That's why I didn't try to face him directly."

"So you had him in sight and still missed your shot?"

Although his first impulse was to defend himself, Galloway couldn't think of a way to do that just then. Instead, he nodded.

The broker shook his head. "I guess you're lucky you're not dead. Didn't he come after you once you were spotted?"

"I don't know. Once I got shot, I got out of there as quickly as I could."

"I'd like to hear that story."

The truth of the matter was that Galloway didn't really remember much about his escape. It was all a mix of pain, panic, movement and instinct. By the time the memories cleared up within his mind, Galloway was stretched out on the ground at his campsite about ten miles from where he'd started.

"I got out of there," Galloway muttered. "That's all that matters."

"I suppose." After taking another sip of his tea, the broker looked around as though he was suddenly bored by the conversation. "Your message said you were hurt."

Reluctantly, Galloway lifted his hand from where it had been resting in his lap. He wore a black glove, which he removed to show the bandages wrapped tightly about his hand and fingers.

The broker leaned in for a closer look, squinting at the section of bandages that were soaked through with dried blood. "Take the bandages off."

"The doctor said I should keep them—"

"Take them off, I said."

Galloway obeyed slowly at first, but then yanked the bandages completely off until they were hanging loosely around his wrist. Once that was done, the bloody nub that had once been his trigger finger was revealed.

"Jesus Christ," the broker mused. "I guess if you needed one more sign that it was time to retire, that sure as hell is it."

"Retire?"

"Well what the hell else should you do? A gunman without a trigger finger is like a stud with no balls. Did you really need me to tell you that?"

Galloway didn't need anyone to tell him that. In fact, he'd been thinking along those same lines from the moment he'd looked down to see what Adams had taken from him. That still didn't help ease the pain any.

"I'll heal," Galloway said. "I'll get better. I'm better now!"

"Yeah? You plan on growing a finger back?"

"I can learn to shoot with my other hand."

"And how long am I supposed to wait?" The broker laughed under his breath. "You were a good prospect, but to be honest I'm glad this happened before I had too much invested in you."

"When I get back up to my prime again, should I contact you at the normal place?"

"Your prime? You're still not getting me. Your prime is over. Your career is over. I've seen men try to shift hands and it never works. They're never the same. Even if you get to be almost as good as you were, that's not what I'm interested in. I only work with the best. There's not a client out there who would pay me good money to hire on some gimp trying to make do with his off-hand."

Galloway nodded slowly as each of the broker's words sunk in like knives being slowly pushed through his flesh, making him wish even more that Adams had been kind enough to just put a bullet through his skull.

"You're finished," the broker said to put the whole matter to rest once and for all. "Don't try to contact me again."

And with that, it was over.

Galloway's career, his livelihood, his future. They were all over and it had been decided after a stray bullet and a cup of tea.

Clint Adams wouldn't get away with it. That's what Galloway vowed after the broker had practically left him for dead in Carson City.

Galloway would see his contract through to prove himself not only as a real professional, but as a man. He wouldn't rest until Clint Adams was dead. After that, Galloway wouldn't only be the most sought-after assassin in the country.

He would be a legend.

TWENTY-FOUR

Galloway sat in his saddle, watching Clint Adams ride out of Brigham Way, picturing him in his sights one more time the way he'd been the first time they'd met. All Galloway had needed to do since that day, if he ever needed to dredge up the part of him that could kill, was think about The Gunsmith.

Of course, Galloway had never needed too much incentive to kill. That had never been the problem. As time passed and he'd healed from his wound, Galloway had been ready to kill just about anyone that crossed his path.

Once he learned to harness that force within him, there seemed to be no limit to the number of people willing to pay for his services. He no longer needed a broker like the one who'd set up his first two professional jobs. Galloway acted as his own broker, sifting through the jobs that would pay the most and lead him in the direction he wanted to go.

Underneath it all, the direction he'd wanted to go was wherever Clint Adams was headed. It didn't matter to Galloway that he'd recovered from what could have been a crippling blow. It didn't matter that he was doing better than ever before in his chosen line of work.

What mattered was that Clint Adams had kept him from

being what he truly could have been. Galloway felt his temperature rise the more he thought about how far he could have gone if he hadn't had to start over again.

It rose into a genuine fever when he thought about how easily Adams had dealt with him.

One shot.

That was all it had taken to put Galloway down. His life had been in Adams's hands at that moment and the only thing that saved him was that he'd fallen beneath the almighty Gunsmith's notice. If anyone else found out about that, his reputation would be tarnished and his career would be over.

But as he watched Adams ride away from town, Galloway knew there was more to it than his career. He could simply let Adams ride off and they could both get on with their lives. Galloway had worked hard to relearn his craft. He'd started over again by picking up a rifle like it was something he'd never seen before and taught himself to be as close as he could get to a marksman.

Galloway had done all those things only because there was a new force spurring him along. There was a new goal set in his mind that overshadowed everything else.

Clint Adams had to pay for what he'd done.

There needed to be a reckoning, or Galloway would never be able to look at himself in the mirror again.

That reckoning had already begun, which made Galloway feel more at peace than he had since before Clint's bullet had separated him from his chosen profession. And the more Galloway thought about what was yet to come, the wider his smile grew upon his face.

TWENTY-FIVE

The hunt was on.

Clint felt that from the moment he'd saddled up and flicked Eclipse's reins. Over the course of his life, Clint had been on both sides of the hunt more times than he could remember. Whether he played the part of predator or prey, there was the same rush of blood through the veins that marked the entire experience.

That rush was what kept the hunters hunting and the prey running. The main difference between those two was sheer force of will. Clint wasn't the type to hunt for the sport of it, but he sure as hell wasn't about to run.

He was always willing to give someone a chance to walk away with their lives, but there was a point when even that option was no longer valid. As far as Clint saw it, whoever was hunting him had refused the civil option when he murdered a defenseless woman while she was still in bed.

That simply wasn't a human thing to do. That was the work of an animal, and the only thing to do to a brutal animal was hunt it down.

As Eclipse thundered over the landscape, Clint held on and stared out at the world that opened up in front of him. He was barely conscious of the horse beneath him or the effort it took to control such a powerful beast. He and Eclipse had ridden over enough miles for them to be able to trust each other.

Clint would search for the animal in question and Eclipse would get him there. After that, the results were anyone's guess.

If this Galloway was the man behind Cassie's death, Clint figured he would find out soon enough. The only thing that concerned him at the moment was the need to at least get a look at who he was after. He couldn't allow Galloway to remain hidden because then it was only a matter of the killer picking his moment to strike.

Clint needed to step the game up a notch and take away the other man's edge.

That meant drawing the hunter out into the open. The one thing Clint was fairly sure of was that whoever the hunter was, he was after him. Therefore, Clint knew that the only way to get the hunter away from any other innocents was to leave town himself.

Seconds ticked into minutes and the minutes had almost piled into an hour with Eclipse still charging across the open trail. Once he got the sense that he was far enough away from Brigham Way, Clint patted Eclipse's neck to let the stallion know that a change would be on its way real soon.

The trail in front of him stretched out into the desert. There were canyons not too far ahead, which meant there was also a much rougher ride in store for anyone charging ahead too recklessly. Even the sky seemed to take on a different hue as the landscape spread out into an open expanse.

Clint didn't have time to admire the scenery, however. He was too busy preparing for a quick maneuver that would give him what he was after. A few more pats on the stallion's neck caught Eclipse's attention. From there, Clint tugged back on the reins and hung on tightly.

The Darley Arabian responded instantly to his rider's

request and slowed almost to a halt after running to his heart's content. With a slight shake of its head and a rumbling snort churning through his nose and throat, Eclipse reared around 180 degrees to face the trail behind him with a fiery gaze.

Clint's eyes were just as intense, but there was a sharpness in them that he'd been building up since he'd left town, honing it like a blade against a whetstone. He knew he might not get much of a chance to accomplish what should have been a simple task.

Then again, getting a look at someone who knew how to keep from being seen wasn't all that simple.

For a moment, Clint felt a scowl come across his face. He didn't see anything behind him apart from familiar terrain and the dust that had been kicked up by Eclipse's hooves. Then, just as he was about to shift his gaze to the trail ahead, something caught his eye. It felt like the first victory of the day.

Someone was behind him all right.

Clint could see the shape of the horse and rider like a mirage. It wasn't much more than a bit of movement at first, but once Clint focused on it he could definitely make out the distinctive shapes he'd been hoping to find.

The rider was good; Clint had to credit him with that much. Almost as soon as he was spotted, the figure in the distance had changed course and dashed for a group of rocks not too far off the trail. But there was too much open space to be covered that quickly, no matter how good of a horse the other man was riding.

And that was exactly what Clint had been counting on when he'd chosen that spot to make his sudden turn.

Giving the reins a subtle flick, Clint backtracked just enough to keep the other rider in his field of vision. It wasn't time to chase him just yet. For the moment, all Clint wanted to do was send a message of his own.

There was no doubt that the rider was watching Clint

very closely. Once he saw Clint was watching him, the other man brought his horse to a stop just short of the rocks and turned to face Clint directly.

They were too far apart for either man to see much by way of details. But the looks on their faces or the color of their eyes wasn't important. What was important was that Clint show that he hadn't been chased out or herded anywhere.

It was now clear that Clint had picked out this spot the moment he'd saddled Eclipse back in town.

Clint stared at the other man, who stared right back at him. Neither man dared to make too sudden of a move, although the stalemate was bound to be broken at any second.

It was a moment that hung by a thread. One or both could start shooting just as easily as they could ride away.

And in that moment, the roles of hunter and prey weren't so easily defined.

TWENTY-SIX

There were plenty of things Clint could do in that single moment. All of them flowed through his mind in the space of a heartbeat and he chose one just as quickly. When it came to the decisions regarding life and death, a man rarely had more time than that to make them. Clint knew that plenty well and figured that the man in the distance possibly knew it even more.

His decision made, Clint didn't give himself enough time to reconsider before he went into action. Keeping low as he took hold of the reins, Clint steered Eclipse away from the man he'd spotted and back in the direction they'd been riding all day long. From there, he touched his heels to the stallion's sides, which got Eclipse moving like he was in a race.

Clint let a second or two pass before taking a quick look behind him. The other man was still there watching. In fact, it looked as though he was moving away from the rocks he'd started to use as shelter so he could watch and see what Clint had up his sleeve.

Clint smirked to himself, knowing he had the other man hooked better than a trout that had swallowed the worm and hook in a single bite. The faster he rode, the more Clint could feel that proverbial line growing taut.

One more look behind was enough to show that to be true since the other rider was now continuing his pursuit.

"Hope you're up to a run today, boy," Clint said as his head remained low against Eclipse's neck. "Because that's exactly what you're going to get."

It had been a little while since Clint had ridden through this part of Nevada. Still, the more ground he covered, the more familiar it became. He'd ridden this very trail more than once, and out that close to the desert, things had a real good habit of staying the same.

Towns didn't boom as much any longer, especially in a land that could be rougher than any mortal enemy. The sun cooked the ground as easily as it cooked anyone walking that ground, making ignorance of how to survive the same as a death sentence.

Clint knew what he was doing, which was exactly why he kept steering away from the more well-worn tracks and putting his back to civilization. Whoever that man was behind him, Clint was about to make sure his hunt was going to be one hell of a trial.

On the same note, Clint was also certain that he wasn't about to lose that hunter anytime soon. It was going to take much more than some rough terrain to shake a man like that. Clint had a good idea of that when he'd seen what had been done to poor Cassie. That notion became a certainty when he'd taken his look at the other man not too long ago.

That one look was more than enough to say a lot of things. Clint could feel the intensity as though there was only an inch or two separating him from the other rider. Whether two men were squaring off on a lonely stretch of desert trail or on a battlefield, that feeling was the same.

Clint used that to his advantage, making sure he gave

the other man one hell of a ride before making the next move in this dangerous game.

Eclipse's hooves pounded against the baked ground like a hammer crashing against the side of a mountain. Every impact rattled Clint and Eclipse to the bone while also pushing them onward. The air started to feel like the breath of a furnace as it rushed past Clint's head. The few deep breaths he could take were like inhaling steam. It burned the back of his throat without doing much to fill his lungs.

Knowing that the Darley Arabian was feeling the same amount of misery or more, Clint patted Eclipse's neck to soothe the stallion's waning spirit. He knew that Eclipse would ride until all four legs broke if that was needed, but Clint wasn't about to mistreat that kind of trust.

For the moment, however, they both needed to put up with the desert and the blazing sun overhead. Perhaps it was more than that, even. Perhaps the elements were some kind of divine punishment for the pain that was to come once both men took their game to the next level.

Clint's arms and legs moved without him having to tell them what to do. They shifted right along with the rest of his body to stay in the saddle as Eclipse charged beneath him. With the history between himself and the Darley Arabian, it wasn't much more than reflex to stay atop the charging stallion.

The trickier part was figuring out exactly where to direct the storm of Eclipse's pounding hooves. Clint's eyes were constantly in motion, flicking back and forth in between the occasional quick glances over his shoulder.

The other rider was still there behind him. In fact, it was even easier to spot him since he needed to push his own horse to the limit just to keep up. Once Clint spotted the second trail of dust in his wake, he turned his attention back toward the increasingly rugged terrain in front of him.

Just as Clint could feel the shifting of Eclipse beneath him, he could feel the twists and turns within the trail itself.

More than just twisting from one side to another, the trail was bucking up and down as well, like a set of jagged ripples frozen forever within the surface of the desert.

For the most part, Eclipse was running fast enough to sail over the bigger slopes. All the stallion needed to do was pick the next spot to place his hooves before pushing up and forward once again. Lather was starting to form on Eclipse's dark coat and the constant effort was starting to wear on the Darley Arabian's resolve.

Clint could feel that as well as the way Eclipse's sides heaved in and out under the saddle like an overworked set of bellows. "Just a little longer," he said even though he knew the stallion couldn't hear much over the pounding of its shoes against the earth. "We're almost there."

The terrain was uneven, rocky and growing more so by the second. One moment, Clint could see a good couple of miles in front of him and in the next, his view was blocked by a rocky slope that seemed to sprout up right in front of him. He'd been steering toward one of the bigger of those slopes and was glad to find a narrow, winding path leading toward the top.

That path was so narrow that it was more suited for walking. It would have been tricky to lead a pack mule along the twisting trail, so riding at close to full gallop was a true test of Clint's horsemanship. By the time he got close to the spot where the trail crested the slope and dropped down over the other side, he was simply hanging on and letting Eclipse do his best to keep his footing.

At the last possible moment, Clint eased back on the reins and slowed Eclipse down. He didn't want to stop too suddenly or they would both slide across the loose gravel and over the top of the slope.

Eclipse responded perfectly, despite the heaving breaths that roared through his flaring nostrils. Turning away from the trail as Clint requested, the Darley Arabian slowed to a trot and then finally to a walk. By the time he came to a stop, Eclipse was panting heavily from a combination of the vigorous run and unforgiving heat.

Clint heard the stallion's labored breathing for all of a second before that sound was swallowed up by the thunder of approaching hooves. His hand dropped reflexively to the pistol at his side and his eyes remained focused on the spot where the trail crested over the top of the slope.

Those hooves came in fast enough that Clint started to wonder if the other man might just charge straight off the side. Just as he was certain he was going to see the other man up close and personal, the thundering hooves turned away and then were silenced altogether.

Clint couldn't believe it.

Straining his ears to pick up even the slightest sound of where the other man had gone, all he got was the rumble inside his own head, the pounding of his heartbeat and the rush of a hot, empty wind.

"Damn," Clint thought as all those sounds faded away. "This guy's better than I figured."

TWENTY-SEVEN

Clint was laying on his belly with his chin pressed against the dirt on top of the rise. Just below him, Eclipse was standing and catching his breath not far from where the two had come to a stop just moments ago. Already the Darley Arabian seemed ready to move but wasn't about to pass up a chance to get some wind back into his sails.

Clint, on the other hand, wasn't so hearty.

The difference between man and animal was clearly pronounced in extreme environments, and they didn't get much more extreme than in the desert. When he thought about how much worse it got the deeper into the desert he went, Clint felt everything inside of him want to head back for the comforts of the nearest town.

Part of that was because of the heat, but an even bigger part was the sun beating directly down onto the back of Clint's head. No matter how much protection he gave himself, Clint knew the sun's rays were especially harsh when there was nothing more than fabric or leather getting in their way. He could feel the heat slicing straight through his clothes like needles that had been left in a fire.

It was no wonder that men quickly lost their minds when stranded in the desert. Already he could feel his lips curling back as the moisture was sucked right out of them. But rather than give in to his instincts, Clint stayed right where he was and waited.

The spot he'd chosen was a rock surface that had been smoothed by the sun. It was the top of the uppermost rock on the slope, rising up about seven or eight feet from where Eclipse was standing. He knew that even though the other rider had stayed out of sight after Clint's abrupt stop, he couldn't have gotten far after that.

Thanks to the barren, rugged terrain, there weren't many places to hide apart from a few narrow crevasses and one or two lips of rock jutting out from the other side of the slope.

Clint could see all of that from his vantage point, which was exactly why he'd chosen it in the first place. When he'd scrambled up to the top of the slope a few minutes ago, he could hear movement coming from not too far away. It was the unmistakable sound of a horse navigating back down the crooked trail, but it didn't last nearly long enough for the other man to have gotten away from the slope entirely.

So, knowing that his enemy was dangerously close, Clint held his precarious ground and waited.

When he'd first brought Eclipse to a stop, Clint's ears might as well have been filled with water. The thunder of Eclipse's hooves had been deafening against the parched earth and the pounding of his own heart was like a hammer within his rib cage.

Now that all of those things had receded, the silence was the thing that filled every one of his senses.

With the heat so thick in the air, the quiet felt like a heavy blanket weighing him down. Every rustle of the wind caught his attention, until such noises became more of a distraction than anything else. Even the rocks around him were so hot that they gave off a distinct, musty scent.

The longer Clint waited, the more all of those things

impressed themselves upon him. Finally, although hardly anything in sight was moving, he felt as if he wanted to stand up and let out a scream just to clear the fog that was filling his head.

But that was exactly what he needed to avoid.

It was just the heat making him feel those things and he needed to do all he could to avoid giving in to it.

Clint thought about the canteen that was hanging from Eclipse's saddle. Although he wasn't about to go get it right then, knowing it was there was enough to comfort him for the moment. Even more, the thought of the water itself trickling down his throat made Clint's racing heart slow down a bit and the haze within his brain start to clear.

Never before had the term "second wind" seemed so appropriate. After that brief pause to calm himself, Clint felt as though he'd woken up from a nap and was ready to sit in that spot for another couple of hours. That eagerness lasted for all of a couple of seconds before being tempered by the unrelenting sun.

Clint knew that no matter how many second winds he got, he couldn't lie with his back to the sun for very much longer. That was a really good way to pass out from heat exhaustion, which was, in turn, the perfect way to die at the hands of whoever was out for his blood.

Just when Clint was about to abandon his post, he was rewarded for all his patience. It seemed that his strength of will had been hardier than the other man's, because he could hear the scrapings of slow, heavy steps drawing closer to the opposite side of the rock.

TWENTY-EIGHT

Clint inched along the top of the rock until he could look over in the proper direction. There wasn't much in that direction apart from the steepest side of the slope and the trail that led down to the desert floor below.

The more Clint moved toward the edge of the rock, the more it felt like he was going to fall right over it. Still, he couldn't allow himself to stop moving until he got a look at what was coming toward him. It was a tenuous situation, however, since missing his glimpse at the other man was just as bad as falling off the rock and breaking his back.

Either way, Clint wound up a dead man.

The stone beneath him offered less for him to hold onto and his sweat-stained shirt made it even harder for him to keep from slipping. Reaching out to grip onto the side of the rock with both hands, Clint was able to peer over the edge until he could look straight down at the source of the approaching steps.

Stretching out to the limits of his reach and his very body, Clint extended himself until he could feel his spine crying out for mercy. His eyes were burning in their sockets, partly due to the heat and partly because of the strain of trying so desperately to see what was coming for him.

All at once, Clint saw what he'd been looking for. The source of the steps wasn't a man, but a horse. What made Clint want to curse out loud was the fact that there was no rider on the horse.

Dropping all attempts to remain silent, Clint pulled himself back onto the slightly rounded surface of the rock and scrambled around so he could face the opposite direction. If there was no rider on that horse, then the animal had been sent up as a distraction. Either that, or the rider had fallen off long ago.

Whichever it was, Clint wasn't gaining anything by trying to keep his position a secret.

His mind raced with the worst possible scenario, which he arrived at by simply putting himself in the other man's boots. If that horse had been sent to draw Clint's attention, then something else was happening that needed to be stopped.

When he shifted around, Clint half-expected to find the other man crawling up the rock to attack him. He didn't see that when he turned around. In fact, he didn't see anything at all. The heavy, imposing silence had returned like an unwelcome visitor.

All he could see when he first looked over the edge of the rock was the Darley Arabian's slowly shifting back. From there, Clint immediately picked out another shape crawling over the parched rock like a lizard on its belly.

The other man wasn't sneaking up on Clint, but had his eye on Eclipse instead. Gripping a hunting knife in hand, he extended the blade toward the Darley Arabian's hind leg while eyeing the tendon running just beneath the horse's skin.

Clint could see the hungry glint in the man's eye as he stretched that blade out to do his damage to Eclipse's leg. Crippling that horse in the middle of such harsh terrain was a sneaky way to impose a death sentence on Clint. More than that, it was a surefire way to make Clint want to wring that man's neck.

No longer worrying about keeping quiet, Clint scrambled over the edge of his rock while giving only a second thought to positioning himself for a proper landing. He was still pivoting his torso when his legs swung out over the side and he pushed off with both hands.

Eclipse had been shifting around to get a look at what was creeping up on his hind legs when he pulled his snout upward to catch a glimpse of Clint dropping down in front of him. The Darley Arabian jumped away to let Clint land safely, which also brought his hind legs closer to Galloway's blade.

Clint made a noise that was part yell and part bark, which exploded from the back of his throat like a forced cough. It was the best noise he could make with such short notice and was intended merely to catch Eclipse's attention while also getting the horse to move.

The noise was completely successful in both regards. Eclipse stared to rear up but also charged forward a few steps to Clint's left.

Gritting his teeth, Galloway put all of his strength into one, vicious swing. He knew he wouldn't be able to do the damage he'd wanted, but he wasn't about to let his efforts go to waste.

At first, he thought his blade was going to catch nothing but air. Then, the knife's edge took a bite out of leathery flesh and sent a fine crimson spray through the air and onto the parched ground. Eclipse let out a pained whinny before rearing up and pumping his front hooves at the air.

Clint ducked low while moving forward so he could avoid getting caught by one of the stallion's shoes. The sound of Eclipse's frantic voice filled Clint's head with a rage all his own, making him feel as though he'd been the one to get cut by that other man's blade.

Moving forward like a charging bull, Clint didn't even grab for his gun before slamming his shoulder into the other man's upper body. He'd seen Galloway straighten up a bit and had even seen the knife coming toward him, but none of that gave Clint a moment's pause.

Galloway almost had the knife switched to a lower grip but was unable to point the blade toward Clint before being tackled. Nearly all the wind was driven from his lungs as Clint's shoulder pounded into his abdomen.

Once Clint felt that he was managing to push the other man backward, he knew he had him. All that was left was to slam him against the closest rock face and show Galloway the business end of a modified Colt revolver.

Being the professional he was, Galloway saw this also. He knew he was moments away from losing the fight, which was why he struck one more time at the only weak spot he'd found. Flipping the knife in his hand until he had a hold of it by the blade, Galloway made sure Clint saw what he was doing before snapping the weapon toward that fine-looking Darley Arabian stallion.

TWENTY-NINE

If Clint had seen the throw just a split second later, he might not have been able to do anything about it. Unfortunately, with the knife already leaving Galloway's hand, there still wasn't much to be done.

Snapping his arm out to get a hold of Galloway was like trying to catch hold of a bullet that had already left the chamber. Even so, Clint did the best he could to at least throw off the man's aim. His forearm pounded into Galloway's elbow from an awkward angle, but the throw had already been made.

For a moment, Clint thought he might be able to catch the knife as it sailed through the air. That hope lasted right up until Clint's fingertips barely nicked the knife's handle and then passed into the spinning weapon's empty wake.

Both of them watched the knife spin toward Eclipse as the steel of the blade caught rays from the sun and reflected them in different directions.

All Clint had to see was the knife draw even more of Eclipse's blood for him to turn his anger directly onto its source. When he shifted his eyes to get a look at Galloway,

Clint could feel a heat rising from within himself that had nothing at all to do with the sun.

It had been a quick toss, but still it managed to catch a piece of its target. Galloway's blade sliced a piece of flesh off of Eclipse's flank. The damage was small, but the wound still caused enough pain to make even the most well-behaved horse lose its composure.

Eclipse reared up again. That pain, combined with the pain from the initial wound, brought the stallion close to a frenzy as it bucked and kicked at what must have felt like hot teeth gnawing into his flesh.

"You yellow son of a bitch," Clint snarled as he lashed out with a vicious uppercut that landed on target.

The punch sent Galloway's head snapping back as blood spurted from the corner of his mouth. Rather than strike back, Galloway rolled with the punch and used its momentum to carry him away from Clint. He landed roughly upon his backside and scooted back on the dusty ground. From there, Galloway scrambled toward a corner formed in the rock that was big enough to use as cover.

Clint vowed he wouldn't let Galloway get to that corner. For the moment, he didn't care about who Galloway was, what had happened between them or why he was hunting him now. All that Clint could think about was that he was after the man who'd been out to maim Eclipse, and that was more than enough to keep him going.

But Galloway was quick enough on his feet to make it around that corner so he could press his back flat up against the rock. Sucking in a deep breath, he drew his gun and waited for Clint to come charging around the corner.

But Clint didn't come.

In fact, the more Galloway strained to hear Clint's footsteps, the more he was mocked by the growing silence.

Galloway wasn't the only one who was able to play hiding games. In fact, Clint had eluded better men than him

with far less effort. Now that he had his back pressed
against his own piece of rock, Clint filled his lungs with air
and held it until his heart began to slow to a somewhat
lesser roar.

Clint's hand remained steady just above the grip of his
Colt, but he kept himself from drawing it. He knew that no
matter how little noise pulling the gun would make, it
would still be more noise than he could afford.

Every move had to be taken into consideration since it
could very well be either man's last. Any mistake could be
a fatal one in a stand-off where each man was just waiting
for an opening in which to strike.

Clint gritted his teeth and let some breath pass from between them. With his back pressed against the rock just
around the corner from where Galloway was standing, he
could almost hear the killer's boots scraping against the
dirt.

There was only a few steps and less than a foot of rock
separating them. If either one decided to reach around the
corner, they would almost immediately realize where the
other was hiding. For that reason, they both kept still and
tried to ignore the impulses urging them to make a charge.

Clint could hear Eclipse fussing noisily not too far
away. The stallion was still upright, but was limping and
fretting on his wounded leg. As much as he wanted to take
a closer look at the Darley Arabian, Clint wasn't about to
give the other man the very chance he'd been hoping for.

Then again, Clint wasn't about to let the other man get
away, either.

Eclipse was bucking and kicking nearby, sending chunks
of dirt and rock through the air. His hooves slammed down
against the ground with a mighty thump before he launched
himself up again once the cycle of pain tore through him
again.

Glancing over to the fretting horse, Clint saw that Eclipse
was getting dangerously close to the edge of the trail that

had led that far up the rise. He knew the stallion well enough to be able to tell when he could leave the horse alone and when he needed to step in.

With blood flowing from his flank as well as his hind leg, Eclipse had been pushed into a frenzy that was about to carry him right over the ledge.

Galloway must have heard this too, since he broke from his cover around the corner and made a run for his own horse, which was waiting for him a little further down the trail. He did his best to keep close to the rocks, but he couldn't rely on that cover beyond a couple of paces.

When Clint heard the footsteps coming from around the corner, he knew it was his last opportunity to get the other man without leaving Eclipse's fate up to chance. Keeping himself low, he stepped around the corner and drew his Colt in one fluid motion.

The moment he cleared the rock, Clint saw that Galloway had gotten even farther away than he'd anticipated. Not only that, but the other man was turning back as well to take aim with his own pistol.

Both men fired their shots simultaneously.

Galloway's pistol erupted in sparks and smoke, sending a round toward where Clint's head would have been if he hadn't ducked before coming into view. Even so, the shot came close enough to send a few rocky splinters into Clint's neck as the bullet ricocheted off the rock.

Clint's shot was equally rushed, but he wasn't running at full speed and turning to fire over his shoulder. The modified Colt sent its lead through the air, hissing toward Galloway and then drilling a hole into his hip. Rather than come out the other side, the hot lead bounced off of one bone before lodging itself in another.

Now, it was Galloway's turn to howl in pain as he spun awkwardly on one foot and then dropped to the ground. Blood spewed from his wound, but that didn't keep him from struggling to get to his horse.

Clint's first impulse was to either disarm Galloway or finish him off. Before he could do anything at all, he heard the pained whinny of a close friend who was about to be in mortal danger.

Eclipse was still bucking from the pain and shock of getting cut by Galloway's blade. Each of his flailing steps brought him closer to the ledge and a fall of at least twenty feet onto an unforgiving desert floor.

Suddenly, Clint had a very important decision to make.

THIRTY

Eclipse was every bit as overheated as Clint had been, with the added strain of having been the one to walk across the desert under the blazing sun. Getting picked apart by Galloway's blade only added to the strain, resulting in the stallion being driven nearly out of his mind.

At least, that's the way it looked to Clint as he rushed over to see if he could calm the Darley Arabian down.

Every step the stallion took brought it closer to dropping over the side. Thinking about that, Clint could already hear the crunch of bones snapping within the horse's body. After that, he would find himself in a serious predicament, being forced to walk to the next town.

He wouldn't be the first to get into such a mess. The desert was filled with the bones of other such unlucky souls.

All of that went through Clint's mind as he rushed toward the bucking stallion. Eclipse's hooves were flying through the air, creating a sound similar to logs being swung at Clint's head. Galloway wasn't forgotten. On the contrary, Clint cursed the other man in the back of his mind for being the one to put Eclipse into harm's way.

"Easy boy," Clint said in a soothing voice that could just

barely be heard over the pounding of hooves against baked rock. "I know you're hurting, but you've got to take it easy. Just listen to me and try to calm down."

At first, the horse's eyes were glazed over and blinking furiously. They looked almost as lifeless as glass, and it was plain to see that Eclipse was panicked and focusing only on the pain stemming from his fresh, bleeding wounds.

One of those powerful hooves lashed out toward Clint's face, but he was able to duck just before getting knocked clean out of his boots. Every one of Clint's senses were being stretched to their limits. He listened to the stallion's breathing as well as the churning of air around Eclipse's hooves.

Clint watched the Darley Arabian's hooves, tracking every snap of their heavy metal shoes. He even watched the muscles tensing in Eclipse's legs for any hint as to which way the horse would kick next. Getting hit by one of those hooves, even by a glancing blow, was not an option since the impact would be powerful enough to knock him unconscious.

There was an equally good chance that such a blow would simply kill Clint outright.

Clint inched closer to the stallion while continuing to talk in a steady, soothing voice.

"Come on now," he said. "You don't want to kill me, do you?"

The closer he got, the more Clint could tell Eclipse was noticing him. Finally, just before the stallion was about to take one more step off the edge, his eyes settled upon the face of his rider.

Clint noticed the glance immediately and locked eyes with the stallion. "That's it," he said, reaching out slowly with one hand. "You know my face well enough. Just come over to me and get away from that ledge."

Although he could see the sun glinting off the blood that

was still wet upon Eclipse's skin, Clint did his best to ignore it. The last thing he needed was to draw Eclipse's attention to the wounds just when he was making some progress.

"That's it, boy. Easy now."

Clint had made it close enough to reach out and pat Eclipse's nose if he wanted to. But the stallion was still fidgeting and nervously inching back toward the drop-off.

Once he knew that he had the stallion's full attention, Clint straightened up and kept his eyes locked with Eclipse's. Dropping his voice to a firm, commanding tone, he said, "Come here, Eclipse. Right now."

After a moment's hesitation, the Darley Arabian let out a shaky breath before lowering his head and stepping forward. All the fight and terror had gone from the stallion, leaving a whole mess of pain in its place. Clint reached out to rub Eclipse's nose before taking hold of the reins and leading him forward.

"That's a good boy. Now let me get a look at you."

Clint checked over the stallion's wounds and found that they weren't too bad once most of the blood was wiped away. Still, the Darley Arabian wasn't about to win any races anytime soon.

With Eclipse calmed down, Clint led the stallion to some shade before drawing his Colt once again.

"Stay here, boy," he said. "I've still got some business to take care of."

THIRTY-ONE

Galloway was nowhere to be found.

Clint's blood was boiling so much within his veins that he almost set out into the desert on foot just to get a shot at the other man. But that was nothing more than a vengeful wish. Cutting into Eclipse was not only a cheap tactic to slow Clint down, it was like tossing a knife at a member of Clint's family.

Even though it was a tough pill to swallow, Clint choked down his desire to feel his hands wrapped around Galloway's throat and turned back to where Eclipse was waiting. The Darley Arabian had fought through the pain and was already making his way down from the rock formation to meet Clint at the bottom.

"Whoa there," Clint said, picking up his speed to meet Eclipse. "Where do you think you're going?"

The stallion looked more tired than anything else and wasn't about to let himself be overtaken by pain again. In fact, if Clint had to hazard a guess, he would even say that the horse had a fire in his eyes similar to the one Clint felt in his own belly.

Reaching out to stroke the damp skin along the stallion's neck, Clint said, "I know, I know. I want to catch up

126

with that bastard too. But first I've got to get a look at those wounds to make sure you don't get worse before I get you some proper care."

Although Clint wasn't much of a horse doctor, he knew enough of the basics to get Eclipse in good enough shape to keep moving. He sifted through his saddlebags to find some rags that he could do without. He tore those rags into strips, soaked them in some water and then wrapped them around Eclipse's bloodied foreleg.

The wound on Eclipse's flank wasn't as easy to wrap, but Clint did the best he could. He needed to rip one of his shirts into additional bandages, but he was more than willing to make the sacrifice. Before too long, the makeshift bandages were tied in place.

The bleeding had stopped for the moment since most of Eclipse's body was thick with either muscle or bone. Galloway's blade hadn't found anything too vital and Clint was damn glad for that bit of luck. Then again, considering that they still had to cover several more miles of desert, perhaps luck wasn't exactly too fitting of a word.

Before heading off again, Clint ran back to where most of the scuffle had taken place. It was easy enough to find the spot due to all the blood that had soaked into the otherwise dry dirt. Finding the knife Galloway had thrown was a bit harder, but Clint managed to catch sight of the weapon thanks to a glint of sunlight off of its blade. Clint picked it up and wiped Eclipse's blood off using his own shirt.

Clint had seen Indians perform simple rituals like marking themselves with the blood of a fallen friend. To them, it could mean anything from a spiritual connection to a pledge for vengeance. For Clint, it was just a way to clean the blade, but it was easy to see why that act could mean so much more.

Looking down at Eclipse's blood on his shirt made Clint feel like he had a permanent reminder of what he needed to do. Although there was no way he was about to forget Galloway anytime soon, he now felt as though some pact had been sealed between them.

Hunter and hunted.

Those titles didn't mean much any more. What mattered was that blood had already been spilled and there was plenty more on the way. Clint was certain of that.

When he got back to where Eclipse was waiting, Clint dropped the knife into his saddle bag and then fished out his spyglass. The telescope was dented from years of use and fit into his hands like the metal had been specially crafted for them.

Lifting the eyepiece, he scanned the horizon for any trace of Galloway. Dust still hung in the air from the man's hasty departure, giving Clint a general notion of which way he'd headed. Before too long, Clint spotted a trace of movement amid another outcropping of rocks.

At least there were a few advantages to being on the outskirts of the desert. First of all, there were next to zero places to hide. If Clint decided to go after Galloway, he knew he could track the man down in a matter of hours no matter how hard Galloway tried to elude him.

He couldn't do that, however, because Eclipse was in need of some better attention than a few ripped bandages that were already soaking through with blood. Clint was in need of some attention himself in the form of water and a cool place to rest for a spell.

That led to the second advantage of the desert. No matter what hardships Clint faced, Galloway was facing the same ones. His horse may have made it through unscathed, but that wouldn't help much once thirst and fatigue set in.

Staring through the spyglass at that trail of dust that dissipated right in front of him, Clint watched what little motion he could find and nodded slowly. A grim certainty set in at that moment. Galloway wasn't about to run away and hide.

The killer had gone through enough trouble to bait Clint

out into the desert and then deal a potentially crippling
blow. Those were just a progression of moves in a deadly
game, not the actions of someone trying to escape.

"I'll be seeing you soon enough," Clint said to himself before lowering the spyglass and dropping it into the saddlebag.

From there, he took hold of Eclipse's reins and rubbed
the horse's neck before climbing gently onto the saddle.
He hated to put strain on the Darley Arabian's wounded
leg, but there wasn't much choice in the matter. Clint was
fairly certain there was a town less than ten miles southwest of where they were and neither of them would make it
if they had to walk at Clint's pace.

Once he was mounted up, Clint flicked the reins and got
Eclipse moving at a steady walk. The stallion was tentative
at first but soon was able to gather some momentum. Already, Clint could see the bandages around Eclipse's leg
were wet with fresh blood.

It was going to be one hell of a long day.

THIRTY-TWO

The town's name was Overlook, Nevada. Surely there was a story or some kind of local legend behind the name, but most folks didn't care to hear it as they made their way down the town's single street. More often than not, visitors who came to Overlook were there to relieve parched throats and rest for a bit until they moved on. Others, however, had somewhat darker motives.

Clint looked to be one of those darker souls when he came walking into town leading his wounded horse by the reins. His skin was cracked from the heat and coated with a thick layer of dirt that had been plastered to him by a sticky film of sweat.

His hands had been closed around the reins for so long that it was difficult for him to open his fist. His eyes gazed out at the world as though he was staring down all of creation. Just then, with nothing but his more primal instincts to see him through the unrelenting heat, he would have been able to cause a hungry grizzly to look the other way.

The sun was low enough on the horizon to give the sky a dark purple hue. What few clouds there were scudded overhead like animals trying to run into their burrows for the night. It had been a long day in general but an even longer one for Clint, who walked up to the first building he could find and knocked on the door.

He could hear some movement on the other side of the door as well as some whispering. When the door was cracked open, Clint barely had the strength to meet the eyes that were staring out at him.

"What is it?" came a voice from inside the little house.

"I need some water," Clint said. "Think you could spare any?"

There was a pause, some hurried words from inside the building and then the eyes peeked through the crack once again. "It's getting on ten o'clock at night."

"I can pay you." When he didn't get much response from that, Clint asked, "Then could you at least tell me where I can find someone to look at my horse? He's been hurt."

"Huh? What're you talking about?" The door opened a bit more so the squat man on the other side could get a look at Eclipse for himself. When his eyes found the Darley Arabian, the nervous man let out a sigh and opened the door enough for Clint to see his whole face. "What happened to your horse?"

"Hurt his leg," Clint replied.

"I see some bandages wrapped on his hind quarter."

Clint nodded. "We got set upon by some bandits. They cut my horse."

"Bandits cut your horse?"

Lifting his gaze so he could look the other man directly in the eyes, Clint said, "That's as far as they got before I ran them off."

The man inside the building looked to be around Clint's age. He had the build and tough skin of a blacksmith, as well as the calloused hands to match. Beads of sweat covered a bald scalp and dripped over a face shadowed by untended stubble. His eyes darted to the blood on Clint's shirt and then back up to Clint's face. Finally, he nodded and opened the door all the way.

"You can come inside for a bit of water," the man said. "But that's it. We've got a man in town who might be able to help with your horse, but you'll have to go to the hotel if you want somewhere to sleep."

"Much obliged," Clint said. "But if it's all the same to you, I'd like to stay out here."

"Oh, sure." Turning to look over his shoulder, the man grumbled, "Myra, bring this man some water. And fetch that bowl from the counter right over there."

Clint didn't move from where he was standing. Part of that was because he was too tired to do much of anything. Another part was because, after walking for the last several miles to get to town, it felt damn good to stand still for a bit.

The squat man stepped aside to let a meek woman in her late twenties step past him. She was carrying a large white wash basin with a bucket of water hanging from her arm.

"This is my wife, Myra," the squat man said. "I'm Alvin."

Myra set the basin down on the edge of her porch and filled it with water. Eclipse stepped right up to it so he could lower his head and lap up the water enthusiastically. She then turned to Clint and held the bucket out to him.

One quick look was all he needed to see the dented tin cup floating on top of the water inside the bucket. Picking up that cup and scooping up some water, Clint dripped some of it onto his parched lips. "My name's Clint Adams," he said while letting out a relieved breath.

Once his lips didn't feel like they were about to crack, Clint took a healthier sip of water. It scorched his throat on the way down, but the pain was like a reminder that he wasn't about to burn up into a lifeless husk after all.

"Where you headed, Clint?" Alvin asked.

"Southwest."

Alvin nodded slowly as he watched Clint fill up on water. There was a suspicion in his eyes, however, that kept him from stepping too far from his wife or the open door to his house. "You with that other one?"

Clint froze with the cup against his lips. His eyes fixed on Alvin as he slowly lowered the cup into the bucket. "What other one?" he asked.

"There was another fella that came through here. Looked to be about in the same bad shape as you."

"Think you could tell me where he was headed?"

Alvin shook his head and reached out to pull his wife back into the house. "I don't know where he went, mister. I saw him come through here looking for water just like you, but he had a wicked look about him."

"Do you know if he's still in town?"

Alvin's eyes flickered toward a spot further down the street as though he thought Galloway was somewhere close by watching him. When he looked back at Clint, the squat man shook his head once and stepped between Clint and his wife. "I don't want any part of that one and I think it's time for you to move along as well."

"You mentioned someone in town that could help my horse," Clint said. "Think you could at least point me in the right direction?"

Suddenly, Alvin looked somewhat ashamed of himself. "Just down the street on the left. Name's Doc Branson. Can't miss his place. There's a shingle hanging outside marking it."

Clint tipped his hat. "Can't thank you enough for the water." Reaching inside his pocket, he took out a silver dollar and handed it over. "Here you go. I said I'd pay you."

"No need for that. Just tell me one thing. Is that other one a friend of yours?"

"No, sir. He's no friend of mine."

"Then watch yourself, because I think I saw him headed for one of the saloons at the other end of town. There's only two and they're right across the street from each other, so I'd suggest you steer clear of them both. You need a drink, you can get it somewhere else."

Although Alvin's tone was clipped and somewhat aggressive, it was plain to see that he intended his words as a warning and not any kind of threat. When he was done speaking, he made sure his wife was inside and then followed her and shut his door.

As far as Clint was concerned, the squat man had done the right thing. Once he and Galloway met up again, the safest place would be behind a locked door and some thick walls.

THIRTY-THREE

Finding Doc Branson's place was just as easy as Alvin had said it would be. The town of Overlook wasn't more than a populated swelling in the road and had obviously been much more at one time or another. For every building that was relatively well maintained, there was another one not too far off that had been allowed to fall over and be covered up by the encroaching desert.

The wind howled with a vengeance, causing even the strongest buildings to creak where they stood. Clint had grown accustomed to harsh treatment from the elements and pushed on down the street just as he'd forced himself to walk all the way into town.

When he got to the building marked by the doctor's shingle, Clint kept hold of the reins and walked right up to the front door. Only a few crooked boards had been laid down on either side of the street, so there was nowhere solid to tie the reins.

Eclipse had been through enough already, Clint figured. There was no need to tie him to some post that might get uprooted at any second.

Clint knocked on the door and waited for a response. When he didn't get one, he made a fist and pounded hard enough to be heard over the tumultuous winds. Eventually, a light flickered to life behind the curtains and made a bobbing path toward the front window.

"If this is about some saloon fight," came a voice from behind the door, "it can wait until morning."

Having gotten used to talking to doors just like he'd grown used to feeling like his throat was about to crack open, Clint said, "I need a doctor for my horse."

Some shuffling steps brought the speaker closer to the door. "Your horse?"

"That's right. He's been bleeding pretty badly. Alvin said you might be able to help me."

The door creaked open an inch or two and a thin fellow wearing little spectacles peered through the opening. "Where's the horse?"

Clint stepped aside so the man could get a better look at Eclipse.

His eyes narrowed from behind his spectacles, but he saw what he needed to see in a few seconds. "All right, then," the man said. "Bring him around back and I'll see what I can do." Shifting his eyes back to Clint, he added, "You don't look too good yourself."

"First thing's first. I'll bring him around to the back."

Clint led Eclipse around the building and heard the door get shut and bolted behind him. The doctor's office was a blessedly small building, which meant that Clint didn't have far to walk to get around it. There was a shack behind the main building where the spindly man with the spectacles was waiting with a lantern in his hand.

"Come on," the man said, waving Clint toward the shack with a few hurried motions. "Looks like that horse is about to fall over."

Clint brought Eclipse into the shack and watched as the bespectacled man came inside with him and shut the door.

"Who might you be?" the man asked.

"Clint Adams."

"I was talking about the horse. Darley Arabian if I'm not mistaken."

Clint smirked a bit, which caused the dirt caked upon his face to crack. "You're not mistaken. His name's Eclipse."

"Fine-looking animal," the man said, reaching out to rub Eclipse's nose. "Why don't you tell me what happened?" After squatting down to get a look at Eclipse's bandaged ankle, he glanced toward Clint and added, "That part was directed to you."

"We ran into a—"

"Before you start in, why don't you have a seat. There's a stool right behind you. I'm Doc Branson, by the way, in case Alvin didn't make proper introductions."

After lowering himself onto the stool, Clint instantly felt more like his old self. As he started to speak, Clint watched Doc Branson carefully peel away Eclipse's bandages so he could get a look at the wounds beneath them.

Every so often, the doctor would dab a cloth into some water from a nearby bucket so he could clean away part of the wound. Although the stallion fidgeted at the feel of pressure against the tender flesh, Eclipse seemed to like the doctor just fine. Seeing that put Clint's own mind to ease as well.

Clint gave a vague account of what had happened to them out on that rock ledge. While he withheld details surrounding Galloway and the business he had with him, Clint stayed as faithful to the truth as possible when it concerned how Eclipse got hurt. That way, he figured he could give the doctor as much help as possible in treating the wounds.

After cleaning off the wound on Eclipse's leg, Doc Branson turned his attention to the nasty flesh wound on the stallion's haunch. It took a bit longer to get the bandages off and clean it, but the doctor didn't seem to have much trouble with it.

As he worked, the doctor nodded in response to what Clint was saying and only asked a few questions to keep him talking. Finally, both wounds were cleaned and he stood up from where he'd pulled up his own stool. "Excuse me a moment," he said. "I need to run in to get some fresh dressings as well as some needles and thread to stitch up that leg."

"What about the other wound?" Clint asked.

Doc Branson shrugged and patted Eclipse gently. "There's not a lot to be done about that apart from keeping it clean and covered. That's going to need to heal up on its own. The good news is that it's just a flesh wound and not too serious. It looks like it was aggravated after it happened, though."

Clint lowered his eyes and said, "I had to ride him until I got close enough to walk the rest of the way into town."

"Well, this close to the desert, you didn't have much choice. If you'd waited any longer, that wound could have gotten a whole lot worse. He's a tough one."

"Will he be in running shape again soon?"

"He'll need plenty of rest and will have to take it easy for a while, but I think he should be back to normal after that."

"That's great news, Doc."

"Now you need to take care of yourself. I'll watch over Eclipse here for the rest of the night. Why don't you get to a hotel?"

"If it's all the same to you, I'd prefer to stay close."

The doctor was about to recommend otherwise, but when he saw the look in Clint's eyes, he knew that would have been useless. "Afraid I don't have as comfortable beds as they do in the hotel. I don't serve breakfast either."

"That's fine by me. I doubt I'll be doing much sleeping anyhow."

"Well then, suit yourself. Should I fix up one of my patient's beds or just fluff up a nice bale of hay for you?"

The joke fell upon deaf ears since Clint had already slumped back against the wall and lowered his hat over his eyes. Doc Branson watched Clint for a moment or two, particularly eyeing the gun hanging from his side. Although he wasn't comfortable with the Colt so close to him, the doctor figured in everything he'd heard Clint tell him before.

"I guess you've been through enough," Doc Branson said. "Might as well sleep where you please. At least that other fella won't be looking for you out here."

THIRTY-FOUR

"Is he still up there?"

Both of the women huddled in the small kitchen of the hotel rushed around each other as if they were trying to wear out the boards beneath their feet in record time. The one who'd just spoken was gray-haired, yet strong enough to lift the kettles and pots from her stove without much effort.

The second woman had light brown hair that was on its way to becoming completely gray as well. She was busy cutting off pieces of bread from a stale loaf and arranging them on a plate next to wedges of cheese.

"Of course he's still up there," the second woman replied. "Where else do you think he's gonna go at this time of night?"

"I don't much care where he goes as long as it's away from here."

"Well don't say that too loud, just in case he decides to come down here and check up on us."

"Did you see the woman he brought up there with him?" the gray-haired woman asked. "I doubt he'll be leaving that room anytime soon."

The woman with the brown hair shook her head and

filled a tall cup with warm water. "Disgraceful. If he wants to behave like that, there's plenty of whorehouses to be found in other towns."

Stirring up the stew she was heating up, the gray-haired woman scoffed under her breath. "Other towns? How long have you lived here?"

"All my life."

"And you don't know what kind of business Pearl runs upstairs from the billiard room?"

The pride that had come across the brown-haired woman's face faded a bit and was quickly replaced by a frown. "Well no matter. I still wish that one upstairs would get the hell out of here. He's probably some no good outlaw on the run."

"Good. That means that someone's probably after him."

The brown-haired woman froze and her eyes suddenly became wide. "You think so? You really think there might be someone after him?"

"If he's an outlaw, I'd say so."

"You mean like a posse?"

"Perhaps. How the hell should I know? Just fetch me a bowl so I can fix his supper and take it up to him. I don't want to think about him any more than I have to. Hopefully, he'll just pay his bill tomorrow morning and leave."

"I doubt he'll pay," the second woman grumbled. "He looks like the thieving sort."

Without another word, the gray-haired woman took the bowl she was handed and scooped in a good portion of stew. From there, she dropped the bowl as well as everything else the ladies had prepared onto a wooden tray and picked the tray up with both hands.

"You want me to come with you?" the brown-haired woman asked.

"No. You'll just find something else to do halfway between here and his door. Just be ready to fetch Earl if you hear any trouble."

"All right," she replied, nodding her head vigorously. "I'll do that."

The gray-haired woman took a deep breath and forced a smile onto her face before leaving the kitchen. She walked up the narrow steps as quickly as she could and didn't stop until she was at the only guest room with a locked door.

Tapping her foot against the door, she said, "I brought your food."

There was some movement from within the room. Leaning in close to the door, the gray-haired woman squinted while concentrating to hear as much as she could of what was happening inside the room. Before she actually pressed her ear against the door, she snapped her head back as the door was pulled open.

Galloway looked like something that had been dragged in from the desert rather than anyone who'd ridden into town. His eyes were feral slits as he looked the older woman up and down.

Shifting uncomfortably on her feet, the woman with the tray gathered herself up and asked, "Should I just leave it here in front of the door?"

The door came open then, but only enough for Galloway to reach for the tray. "Thanks, ma'am. I appreciate you being so accommodating so late at night."

"It's not that late. You only missed dinner by a few hours."

"Well, thanks all the same." With that, Galloway reached out and took hold of the tray.

The gray-haired woman took a quick peek around him and was just able to catch a glimpse of someone else inside his room. Her distaste for the situation was strong enough to make her look as if she'd smelled something bad. Just as Galloway was shutting the door, she spoke up.

"Um, is that your wife?"

Galloway stopped and looked at the older woman with disbelief written across his face. "Excuse me?"

"If that's your wife, I can arrange to have a place set for

her at breakfast. If not . . . well . . . this really isn't the sort of hotel that caters to—"

"Don't worry about who she is," Galloway interrupted. "She's keeping me company for the evening and won't be around for breakfast."

The door slammed shut and the latch clattered into place, leaving the old woman standing alone in the hall. She still had her finger raised and her mouth open, but no longer had anyone to scold. Grumbling a few choice words, she turned and walked back down the stairs and to the kitchen.

The brown-haired woman was waiting for her, brewing a kettle of hot water so they could have their nightly tea.

"Was there someone up there with him?" the second woman asked.

"Sure enough."

"Do you know who it was?"

Letting out a short breath, the gray-haired woman snatched a pair of cups that were hanging over a small table in the corner. "Just some whore from down the street."

"They're not supposed to come here."

"I know that, but they'll go wherever they can so long as some man dangles enough money in front of them. I don't want to think about either of them. Let's just have our tea."

THIRTY-FIVE

Clint woke up the next morning feeling as though he'd slept in a barn. When he stretched his arms while opening his eyes, he realized there was a very good reason for feeling like that.

He was in a barn.

With every bone and muscle aching, Clint found it more difficult than normal to clear the sleepiness from his head. Standing up and working some of the kinks out helped a bit, but not as much as seeing Eclipse nearby looking twice as better as he had when the doctor had tended to his wounds.

"Morning, boy," Clint said, reaching out to pat Eclipse on the neck. But he stopped before touching the stallion since he could now see that Eclipse was still asleep.

Letting the Darley Arabian rest for a while longer, Clint opened the door and stepped outside as quietly as he could. The door swung on rusty hinges but held in place solidly enough. Where the building had looked like nothing more than a shack the previous night, Clint could now see that it was a small barn complete with a miniature loft just big enough to store some supplies.

Still groggy from falling asleep on a stool and leaning

against a wall, Clint pulled in a few breaths that began to wake him up from the inside. His eyes snapped open and his hand flashed toward his Colt when he heard a sudden, loud sound come from just out of his line of sight.

When Clint turned to get a look at what had caused that sound, he spotted Doc Branson standing at a large stump with an axe in hand. He'd just split one log and was reaching for another when he saw Clint standing outside the shack.

"Good morning," the doctor said with a wave. "How'd you sleep?"

"It was a rough night," Clint admitted as he walked over to where the doctor was standing. "But it could have been a whole lot worse. Thanks for all your help."

"It's what I do for a living."

"Whatever I owe you, just let me know and I'll be glad to pay."

"Actually, we might be able to work out a deal. You think you could chop some firewood for me? It'd do wonders in working out those kinks in your shoulders and back."

"You saw me limping out here, huh?"

The doctor laughed as he drove the axe's blade into the stump. "No, but you slept in a barn. I've done so enough times to know that it isn't exactly the most comfortable way to spend a night."

Clint stepped over to the stump and pulled the axe out from where it had been stuck. He found the stack of logs to be split, set one upon the stump and got to work.

"How's that stallion of yours?" the doctor asked.

"He looks good," Clint replied, splitting a third off the log in front of him. "Still a bit tired, but good."

"I told you he'll need rest."

Hefting the axe up over his head, Clint swung it down and cut the remaining chunk of wood in half. "It's been a while since I've cut firewood."

"Too much fancy living?"

"That's not a bad problem to have, but that's not exactly my case. Just too busy riding I guess." Placing another log onto the stump, Clint swung the axe up and brought it down relatively close to center. "Either riding or taking care of some other business that always crops up."

"Yeah," the doctor said, glancing at the Colt on Clint's hip. "I can imagine."

Doc Branson watched Clint split a few more logs and then started shifting from one foot to another. "I didn't get to talk to you much last night and there's something I've been meaning to ask."

The effort of picking up the wood from its pile and swinging the axe was truly doing wonders for Clint's muscles. Already, he was feeling heat pulsing through him instead of just the dry heat baking into his skin. "I'll do my best to answer."

"Did you come into town alone?" the doctor asked, wincing as the axe chopped through another log and bit into the stump beneath it. "Or was there someone else on the run after you got ambushed by them bandits?"

Pausing for a moment, Clint took his time finding another log and setting it perfectly into place. He could tell by the tone in the doctor's voice that he wasn't exactly buying the story about the bandits. That meant either Clint's poker face was slipping or Branson knew more than what he was letting on.

"What makes you ask that, Doc? Did someone else come charging in from the desert last night?"

"I'm not sure. Being as we're so close to the desert, plenty of folks come through Overlook."

This time, Clint was the one who wasn't buying what he was being told. But rather than call the doctor on it right away, he simply nodded and got back to his work. "Well, the man who cut up my horse was headed this way the last time I saw him. If he was in town, I'd sure like to know."

Clint hefted the axe over his head and swung it down to a point dead center of the log in front of him. Both halves flew apart and landed among the others laying on the ground. "He was shot," Clint announced. "In the hip. I'd be surprised if he didn't try to get someone to take a look at a wound like that. Are there any other doctors in town?"

Branson shook his head while slowly lowering his eyes. "No. There's not any other doctors in town. Not for miles."

Clint sent the axe deep into the log and all the way through. The blade went through so quickly, that it left the split wood standing on top of the stump. "Then that leaves you."

"You seem like a good man," Branson said. "I'd hate to see anything happen to you by chasing after a dangerous person like that other one."

"Then maybe you shouldn't worry so much."

"And why not?"

"Because I might just be more dangerous than that sorry bastard that came through here before."

THIRTY-SIX

It turned out that Doc Branson didn't have a whole lot else to say. What he did tell Clint was enough to let him know that he hadn't been wasting his time chopping wood behind the doctor's office.

"It was a few hours before you arrived," Branson said. "Some fella came knocking on my door, covered in dirt and soaked with blood. He was a sorry sight but still looked as though he was about a breath away from knocking me on my ass.

"I've seen plenty like that one. Gunmen," Branson said, spitting the word out as though it was an obscenity. "Outlaws who come through here trying to get to Mexico or just to some hole in the middle of the desert where they can't be found. That's the problem with being on the edge of the desert like we are. Some think of us as an oasis and others see us as a last chance to grab what they can before heading into the fire."

Clint nodded, taking in the doctor's words while still chopping the pile of logs. "Did he give you his name?"

The doctor laughed under his breath while waving his hand as if shooing away a fly. "He gave me some name or other, but I knew it wasn't real. By the looks of him, he'd been riding or fighting all day and was too tired to be much of a liar."

"And he was shot?"

"Yep. In the hip, just like you said. Nasty wound. The bullet was lodged in the bone, but I managed to dig it out. I wanted him to stay here and keep off his feet, but he threw me some money and headed out."

"Out of town?" Clint asked.

"Maybe. Although I don't think he could make it too far on that wounded hip of his. Tell you the truth, I was glad to see him go." Branson stared at a spot on the ground and chewed nervously on his bottom lip. "He paid me double my normal fee. Told me to keep the rest as long as I kept my mouth shut about seeing him. Guess I should give that part of the money back, huh?"

"Keep it," Clint said, focusing on the log he'd just taken before driving the axe straight through it. "He won't be needing it."

"Are you . . . are you outlaws?" Branson asked, his nervousness finally swelling up like a frog in his throat.

Clint looked over to the other man. "What do you think?"

"If you were the law, you'd have said so by now. Thing is, we don't have a regular lawman that lives in town. There's a few that ride by to check on us, but most of the time we have to fend for ourselves."

"Well, I'm no lawman," Clint said. "But I can tell you for certain that I'm not an outlaw, either."

"I thought as much. Folks in Overlook have gotten real good at being able to spot the dangerous types pretty quickly."

"I guess you'd have to, seeing as how there's no law out here." Clint slammed the axe through another log and hefted it onto his shoulder. "I'd even wager that you've learned plenty about me already just by watching me so far."

Doc Branson nodded. "I have. That's exactly why I'm not sure whether or not I should say anything else about that other fella. Staying away from him would be the best bet. You'd probably stay out of trouble that way as well."

"Too late for that."

"Then I'm afraid I don't have much else to tell you. When that gunman left here, he headed off down the street toward the other end of town. There's two saloons and just as many hotels that way. There's also a billiards room, but that's mostly known for the ladies that lounge about, if you catch my meaning."

"I do."

"If you're looking to catch up with any stranger that passed through here, I'd say your best bet is to check in with them ladies at the billiard room. They keep their eyes and ears open for strangers that come to town. It's how they earn their living after all."

After picking up one more log, Clint chopped it in two and left the axe sticking out of the top of the stump. It just so happened that that log was also the last from the pile. "I appreciate all you've done. I hope it's all right if Eclipse stays with you for a bit longer."

"I'd insist on that. He's a fine horse and I wouldn't want to tear those stitches open."

"Here," Clint said, holding out some money that he'd taken from his shirt pocket. "This is for services rendered."

"You held up your end," Branson said, pointing toward the twin piles of split wood.

"Then at least take some to cover Eclipse's stay or food or something." Extending his hand, Clint let his exasperation show through in his voice. "Just take it. Please."

The doctor took the money and tucked it away into his pocket. "That fella isn't a bandit."

"No. He isn't."

"He's a killer. I've patched up enough bullet wounds to recognize that cold look in a killer's eyes. They're usually the ones to get shot up or are nearby when someone gets shot."

Clint knew that look all too well.

"But there was something else about that one," Branson continued. "He came to my door with something else in his eyes besides that cold killer's glare. He looked . . . determined, I guess." Taking a moment to think over those words, the doctor finally nodded. "That's it. He was determined. He was after something and as soon as he left, I knew that something was a person. Kind of like . . ." Trailing off, the doctor seemed to know what he wanted to say but couldn't quite put the proper word to it.

"Like a hunter," Clint said.

The doctor snapped his fingers and nodded. "That's it. He looked like a hunter who had his sights set on his target and wasn't about to be distracted. That's all that could get him to walk up to my door with that bullet in his hip. Even when I dug that bullet out of him, he barely made a sound. I watched him to see if he was going to pass out, but he was staring so hard at the wall that I could barely stand to look.

"The truth is that I didn't want to know what he was thinking then and I don't want to know now. The only reason I'm telling you this is that you should know what you're dealing with if you intend to go after an animal like that."

"Thanks," Clint said as he turned and put the doctor behind him. "But I know well enough what kind of man he is."

THIRTY-SEVEN

Clint had no real way of knowing if Galloway was still in town or had already moved on to somewhere else. What he did know was that he couldn't exactly leave town himself since it would be a while before Eclipse was up to the task. After what Galloway had tried to do before, Clint didn't want to take the chance of leaving Eclipse alone long enough for that maniac to finish what he'd started.

If Galloway was trying to settle a personal score, it was more than likely that he would try at least one more time to kill Eclipse. That would be the sort of thing a man would do out of spite, and Galloway had already proven that he was plenty cold enough to think along those lines.

Clint also knew that Galloway was cold enough to murder innocent people for information as well as to prove a point. If DelToro's account was true, then Galloway had slit someone's throat just to be pointed in Clint's general direction.

Just thinking about all of that made Clint's stomach turn. It made him feel like he was choosing the wrong path no matter which way he was leaning.

If he stayed in town, he might be allowing Galloway to

get out ahead of him where he could cause some more damage in another place.

If he left to track Galloway down or even draw him out of Overlook, Clint might be allowing the killer to stay put and kill Eclipse as well as any number of locals just to give Clint something horrible to see when he got back.

Any one of those possibilities were real enough, leaving Clint with only one thing to go by: his instinct.

For the moment, Clint's instinct was to stay in town. With Galloway being hurt, he wouldn't be able to get too far even if he did decide to head out on his own. And if Galloway did leave, he would have to hole up somewhere to heal before he was able to do much of anything else.

Clint needed to stay close to Eclipse and make sure the stallion was able to rest up in peace. That Darley Arabian had pulled him out of more scrapes than he could name and that had to count for something.

Once that was decided, Clint felt a little better about everything in general. His problems were a long ways from being over, but at least he had a plan of action. Just then, his plan was to search the town of Overlook from top to bottom for any trace of Galloway.

If he didn't find the other man, Clint vowed to at least get an idea of where Galloway was headed. Given all the locals who were used to looking out for each other, Clint figured he had to come up with something. Since he didn't have any reason to doubt the doctor's word on the matter, Clint decided to heed Branson's advice and head for the billiard hall.

The place was right where Branson said it would be: down the street and a ways from the saloons. It was a tall, narrow building marked with a sign whose paint was faded from too much sun. Clint had almost forgotten about what time of day it was until he realized that the streets were not only empty but almost perfectly quiet as well.

It was the special kind of quiet that could be found only in the morning's earliest hours. Not much was stirring in Overlook, and the souls that were awake were still doing their best to keep from waking the others. Clint stepped up to the billiard hall and tried the door.

It was locked.

When he attempted to peek through the window along-side the door, he found his view was blocked by some velvet curtains that had been drawn over the glass. Stepping back to take a look at the rest of the street, Clint found plenty more of the same. Even the wind seemed lonely as it tossed about a few clouds of dust or batted around a stray tumbleweed.

Saloons in bigger towns often stayed open all day long, but Clint had his doubts as he walked up to each of the two saloons Overlook had to offer. Sure enough, neither of the saloons were open. Although there were some people inside, they either didn't see Clint waving at them through the window or ignored him so they could get their work done before opening for the day.

That left the next best bet available to Clint, which were the hotels. Unlike saloons, hotels had to stay open all day long. They were also the very spot that Clint would figure Galloway to be after the trials from the day before.

Of course, it wasn't as easy to get people to talk about who came and went in hotels as it was in saloons. But since Clint didn't have many other choices, he turned and started walking toward the closest hotel he'd seen.

That one seemed even more empty than the streets and had only one lonely man to work the front desk. Clint barely got a word out before he could tell that the man was going to be no help whatsoever. He had a sleepiness in his eyes that made it obvious he would barely even remember Clint's face ten seconds after he left. Recalling a customer from the previous night would be a gamble.

Sure enough, half a conversation was all it took for

Clint to turn around and leave the hotel. At least he'd gotten a look at the register before leaving. The most recent signature in that book was from three days ago and the inside of the place had felt deader than a desert night.

Clint's spirits were dropping and even the brightening sunlight couldn't bring them up again. As he stepped outside, the streets were coming alive somewhat and locals were beginning to poke their heads outside.

Clint wasn't feeling half as chipper as the folks he passed and by the time he stepped into the second hotel, he was downright annoyed. Of course, the grumbling in his belly wasn't helping matters at all.

"Hello there," Clint said, forcing a smile onto his face as he walked up to a young, bright-eyed woman standing near the front desk. "I was wondering if you could spare a moment?"

The woman had long, coppery blond hair and the richly tanned skin of someone who'd lived in the desert heat her entire life. When she turned to look at him, she showed Clint a somewhat worried glance. Doing her best to return his smile, she asked, "What can I do for you?"

"I'm looking for someone who might have checked in last night. He's about my height with a light complexion. Smooth face. He probably wasn't looking too good when he—"

"He's gone," she said in a clipped tone.

Clint could see the fear in her eyes and knew that she was just the woman he'd been hoping to find.

THIRTY-EIGHT

The color had drained from the blond woman's face and she even started to back away from Clint as he approached her.

"You've seen the man I described?" he asked.

"Yeah, and I told you he's gone. Wherever he went, I hope he stays there. Are . . . are you a friend of his?"

"No," Clint replied. He noticed the immediate relief that brought to her face. "But I was hoping you might tell me what happened when you saw him."

"It was last night, just as I was about to go home. He came in and his clothes were all bloody. He wore a gun and he stormed in here like he owned the place. He said he wanted a room and some company for the night, so I rented him a room but told him he would have to find his own company."

As the blonde spoke, her words came out faster and faster as if she was glad to be rid of them. Then again, judging by the way she looked at Clint, he was the one she truly wanted to get rid of.

Clint held his hands out to his sides and spoke in a soothing voice. "I'm no friend of his, so you don't have to worry. All I'm after is any help I can get in finding him so I can put him away."

The blonde looked at him as though she was only just starting to listen to his words. "Really?"

"Really."

She let out a breath and walked toward the front door. "Then can we get out of here? I'd rather talk about it where I know nobody else can hear."

Clint agreed to that and soon found himself being led outside. Only another few minutes had passed, but it seemed that the rest of the town was coming out as well now that the blonde had decided to show her face. There were more people walking down the streets and more storefronts were being opened for business.

The blonde was obviously more comfortable now that she was in the open. In fact, the smile on her face was warm and comforting as she extended her hand. "My name is Jolene, by the way. Sorry if I was a bit rude back there."

"Don't give it a thought. I'm Clint Adams."

He shook her hand and saw only a faint trace of recognition in her eyes. Plenty of folks had heard Clint's name, but most of that was because of all the wild rumors and stories out there about him. Rather than remind her that she might have heard about him in a saloon or in a yellowback novel somewhere, Clint moved on.

"So was that the last you saw of him?"

Jolene's smile faded a bit and she nodded. "Yes."

"And what else did he have to say?"

"Only that I should let him know if anyone came looking for him and that if I talked to anyone looking for him that he . . . that he would . . . kill me. Or worse." A shudder worked through her and she looked uncomfortable even though they were standing out in the open. "Maybe I shouldn't be saying any of this."

Clint stopped at the corner, making sure that he could still see the hotel. "You did the right thing. Now, do you know if he's still there?"

"It's like I said before. He's gone."

"Gone for the day or did he head out of town?"

"I don't know," she answered quickly, wrapping her arms around herself as if for protection. "He's just gone."

"Then can you at least tell me which room he was in?"

Jolene thought about it for a while before finally nodding. "Second door on the left. He wanted to be overlooking this street."

"All right then. Maybe you should wait somewhere else while I go check it out."

Her eyes went wide at the sound of that and she shook her head. "Oh no, you don't. Whether you're a man I can trust or not, I'd rather take my chances with you than with him."

"I won't let him get to you."

"And if he's not in his room, will you know for certain where he's at?" Jolene waited for a moment and when she saw that Clint didn't have an answer right away, she reached out and took hold of his arm. "That's what I thought. I'm staying right with you, Clint Adams."

"Are you sure about that?"

She nodded without a moment's hesitation. "I've heard of you from my cousins who used to live in Tombstone and if you can't protect me, then nobody can."

Although Clint had mixed feelings about having his name bandied about in nearly every saloon across the country, he couldn't exactly fault Jolene for her logic. Besides, he didn't want to waste any more time arguing when Galloway could be skulking about at that very moment.

"All right, fine," Clint said. "You can come with me, but stay behind me. If something does happen, I don't want you getting in harm's way or mine for that matter. You understand?"

Jolene nodded. Although she loosened her grip on Clint's arm, she wasn't about to let him go.

They hadn't put much space between themselves and the hotel, but the walk back to that building seemed awfully long. Clint expected an attack to come at any time. Thinking that Galloway was still in town also made him hope that Eclipse was still safe locked away behind the doctor's office.

Clint stepped into the hotel and although he didn't have his gun drawn just yet, his hand was hovering over the Colt. Jolene was right behind him and doing a good job of staying there.

The hotel was quiet. It was so quiet that the silence seemed to fill Clint's ears like water.

"That door," Jolene whispered, pointing to a door that was half open behind the desk. "That was closed the last time I checked."

"Is there anyone else here?"

"Not someone that would have access to the room with the lockbox."

Clint didn't like the sound of that one bit. He also didn't like the sight of a body laying prone on the floor of that neighboring room.

THIRTY-NINE

Clint reached back to take hold of Jolene with his left hand. All he wanted was the feel of her arm, hand or clothing so he could keep track of where she was as he made his way toward the front desk. The moment his fingers found the fabric of her skirt, they closed around it tightly and made sure she stayed behind him.

Moving in a smooth rhythm, Clint's body hunkered down low while also shifting into a sideways stance. That way, as he made it around the desk and went for the door, he wasn't presenting much of a target for whoever was on the other side.

Clint's hand was still over his gun. He didn't want to draw just yet in case there was someone else in there who was just as frightened as Jolene. Nudging the door open with the toe of his boot, Clint took a look inside the room.

The room was a size somewhere between a guest's room and a closet. There wasn't anything in there besides a few cabinets, a small table, a chair and some boxes stacked in one corner. The air was thick with dust and the smell of fresh death.

That brought Clint's eyes to the body on the floor.

Jolene must have spotted it at the same time, because she let out a gasp and tried to rush past him to get into the room.

"Oh my lord," Jolene sobbed. "Mrs. Parrish!"

"Stay back, Jolene," Clint ordered. "Let me get a look around here first."

Unfortunately, there really wasn't much for Clint to see. Apart from the body, everything else in the room was in plain sight. The cabinets had all been forced open, and even the crates had been cracked and ransacked by whomever had last been in that room.

"You said there was a lockbox kept in here?" Clint asked.

Jolene was crying, but she managed to nod when Clint looked back at her. "Over there," she said, pointing to one of the opened cabinets. "It should be in that one over there."

Clint didn't have to spend much time looking to know that the lockbox had been taken. He also didn't have to look at Mrs. Parrish on the floor to know that she was long gone as well.

The gray-haired old woman looked like she couldn't have possibly harmed a fly. Her hands were reaching for the door to the lobby and her eyes were locked open in a mask of fear that was now permanently etched onto her face.

"Do you know this woman?" Clint asked.

Jolene had her hands over her mouth, which seemed to be the only thing keeping her from breaking down completely. She nodded slowly, unable to take her eyes off of the dead woman's face.

"She worked here last night," Jolene explained. "She cooked and cleaned and ran the place sometimes. I heard that she was upset about some woman that was in that man's room, but that was it."

Reaching down to touch the old woman's cheek, Clint's suspicion was confirmed. "She's still warm. This must have just happened."

As if on cue, there was a sound coming from upstairs. Clint heard it and immediately pulled Jolene into the room so he could head back into the lobby. The instant he stuck his head out to take a look, he spotted a familiar face looking down at him from the top of the stairs.

Galloway froze there for a moment. Even though his gun was around his waist, it seemed like it was miles away.

Clint froze as well, knowing that any movement either man made would be the spark to ignite the powder keg. Just then, he spotted something in the crook of Galloway's left arm that put everything together for him.

"Where you going with that lockbox?" Clint asked.

Galloway smirked a bit and replied, "Why you asking? Do you need the money to buy a new horse?"

Rather than let the comment get to him, Clint took a moment to observe everything he could about his surroundings. Thankfully, there wasn't anyone else to get in his way. From this angle, however, he could see a shotgun resting behind the front desk.

"Who's that with you, Adams?" Galloway asked. "She looks like a tasty one. I'll bet she's a hell of a lot better than that old bat I found in the back room there when I was making my withdrawal."

Before Clint could respond, he heard a few hurried footsteps come from behind him. Jolene rushed past him quicker than Clint would have expected, which was why she slipped past him before he could grab her arm.

"You murdering son of a bitch!" Jolene shouted as she ran to the front desk. "I'll kill you!"

Galloway smiled and waited until Jolene had stepped completely in front of Clint before reaching for the gun at his side. He would have made the draw with ease, but the pain from his wound caused him to pause slightly before taking his shot.

With his left hand, Clint reached out to shove Jolene to one side. His right hand was already filled with the modified Colt by the time his line of sight was cleared. Bringing up the pistol, he pointed it like he would point his own finger and squeezed the trigger.

The Colt barked once, spewing a gout of smoke and sparks. Galloway reflexively ducked down as the banister in front of him exploded with a shower of splinters. He tried to return fire but found the banister was as much in his way as it had been in Clint's. He fired off a shot anyhow, but only to cover himself as he charged down the stairs.

Clint went to cut the man off but almost tripped over Jolene as she covered her head with her hands and tried to make it into the back room. She let out a frightened scream while bumping into Clint and then finally started to drop down right where she stood.

Before she could curl herself up into a ball, Clint took hold of her by one arm and nearly lifted her clean off her feet. As soon as he pulled her away from the desk, he fired another shot toward Galloway, who was hobbling down the stairs as fast as his wounded hip would allow.

The Colt sent another round through the air, but Clint hardly expected to hit much of anything. Galloway was moving so awkwardly that it was almost impossible to guess which way he would waver next. He seemed about to fall with every step but maintained a tight enough grip of the banister to keep from doing so.

Just as Clint was going to take a moment to aim, he saw Galloway bring his own gun to bear and fire off another shot.

Jolene tried to scream, but the sound was caught in the back of her throat. All she managed to do was grit her teeth

and clench her eyes tightly shut. The only problem with
that was that she still wasn't in the back room and was
therefore still in the line of fire.

"Stay down!" Clint shouted.

When he looked up again, however, Galloway was already forcing open the door. The man shifted so he could
back out of the door while pulling his trigger as quickly as
he could.

The air seemed to explode around Clint's ears as round
after round was fired at him. He wanted to stand his ground
and put Galloway down, but the killer's first shot had been
close and the rest were only getting closer.

Swearing under his breath, Clint dropped down behind
the desk and covered Jolene with his body. The last shot
came and was followed by the loud slam of the front door.

"Are you all right?" Clint asked.

Jolene had tears streaming down her face but nodded all
the same. "I'm fine. Just go after him. Don't worry about
me!"

Clint pushed off with both legs so he was able to launch
himself onto and over the desk in one mighty leap. Using
his free hand to steady himself against the desk, he
dropped down on the other side and began rushing for the
door, which was still rattling upon it hinges.

He pulled the door open but not until his back was already pressed against the wall beside it. When no shots
were fired at him, Clint hopped into the doorway while
dropping down to a one-kneed firing stance.

Galloway was nowhere to be found.

At first, all Clint could see was a street filled with nothing but confused locals who were still looking around as if
a demon had just flown past them. It wasn't long before
Clint spotted a trail of dust that had been kicked up on the
street. That was also when he heard the sound of a horse's
hooves beating a path away from the hotel.

Clint's first impulse was to jump onto Eclipse's back

and give chase. But Eclipse wasn't there and even if he was, he was in no condition to chase anyone. As much as Clint hated to admit it, Galloway had won another round in their deadly game of cat and mouse.

FORTY

Jolene rushed out to meet Clint but stopped in the doorway. "Is he gone?" she asked.

Although Clint was so frustrated that he could taste the bitterness of it in his throat, he holstered his Colt and nodded. "Yeah. He's gone."

"Where'd he go?"

"I'm sure he's not going too far. Probably just somewhere safe where he can lick his wounds. I'm guessing that's why he went through so much trouble to get the money in that lockbox."

"Are you going after him?"

"I can't. I've got to stay here for a while yet."

Taking a deep breath, Jolene extended her hand and said, "Then you're going to stay somewhere safe. Come on."

At that moment, Cassie's face came into Clint's mind. She was the last woman Galloway had seen him with and now she was dead. Although Clint didn't want to drag Jolene into this any deeper, he was certain that Galloway would love to bury another woman in Clint's life just out of spite.

Once Galloway's horse was out of sight, everyone on the street was starting to turn and look at Clint. "Just a moment," he said to Jolene. "Someone needs to know about what happened to the woman in there."

"What woman?" asked a man in his late fifties who stepped out of the gathering crowd.

Since there was no law in Overlook, Clint walked up to the man who'd stepped forward and explained the situation. Before he was done, another woman with light brown hair emerged from the hotel and nodded solemnly.

"I saw that killer leave here after stealing the money," she said. "I saw it all."

It didn't take long for Clint to relay the grim details of what had happened. Thankfully, the brown-haired woman backed up what he said and was also frightened enough of Galloway that she praised Clint for driving him out.

The local man insisted on having a look for himself, which was Clint's cue to leave with Jolene. Rather than take the chance of Galloway coming back to repay her for talking about him, Clint decided to take Jolene up on her offer. At the very least, it would allow him to stay somewhere unknown to Galloway while also keeping an eye on Jolene. Despite the fact that he knew better, Clint couldn't help but feel that he was the one running away.

It killed him to let Galloway get away, but he also knew that the killer would be back soon enough. DelToro had been right about one thing. Galloway was after Clint's head and wouldn't stop until he got it. If Clint took up the hunt once Eclipse was better, he would also force Galloway to do the same.

Galloway's idea of hunting was torturing people for information and then killing them. Although staying in one place didn't seem like the best idea, it would keep Galloway from questioning anyone else about where he'd gone and it was a hell of a lot better than running.

Jolene was staying in a little cabin just outside of town. Overlook was so small that just about anything not on one of its streets was outside of town. From the cabin, Clint could keep an eye on most of the town. More important, he could see the little barn behind the doctor's office where Eclipse was getting some well-earned rest.

The day had passed with only a few people coming to the cabin to ask about what had happened in the hotel. They didn't want to talk to Jolene and were even more wary of Clint, but they listened to what he had to say. Finally, Clint found himself staring out the window, watching the sun set behind the town's uneven horizon.

"I don't think he's coming back," Jolene said from the area of the cabin that contained the stove and a small, rickety table. "It looked to me like he just wanted to get out of here."

"He'll be back," Clint said with certainty.

Jolene walked away from the soup she was stirring and over to Clint. Kneeling beside him, she placed her hand on his knee and said, "But probably not for a while. Don't you think? That Galloway person could barely make it down the stairs. He's probably trying to find another doctor somewhere."

Plenty had been going through Clint's mind as he'd looked through that glass pane. Most of it had to do with Galloway, but some of it had to do with more immediate concerns. Before too long of a pause, he forced a grin onto his face and said, "You're right. He's still hurting too much to come after me tonight."

"You're about to drop over, Clint. At least have something to eat."

The smell of the soup had already drifted into Clint's part of the cabin and was making his stomach howl angrily within him. "It feels like a hell of a long time since I had a good meal."

"Then have one now. I made it especially for you."

"Actually, it does smell pretty good."

Jolene smiled and stood up. "Come on," she said, taking

Clint's hand. "Folks in this town know how to take care of themselves. I'm sure someone will come get you the moment that murderer shows his face around here."

"You're right. Besides, it's not like anything will happen any quicker just because I'm watching for it."

Although Clint was putting on an amicable facade for Jolene's sake, there was still plenty that didn't sit too well with him. He didn't mention any of that while they ate and he didn't even say much as she cleaned up and lit the few lanterns inside the cabin.

Clint most certainly didn't say anything when he slipped out through the front door while Jolene was curled up asleep on the bed. He had something very important to do and if his instincts were still to be trusted, there was precious little time to spare.

FORTY-ONE

Clint opened the cabin door less than half an hour later so he could slip back inside. Even before he dropped the latch back into place, he heard Jolene's voice from the other side of the room.

"Where did you go?" she asked.

The lanterns had been turned down to a barely visible glow, which was just enough for Clint to see the worry on her face. Jolene sat bolt upright in her bed, clutching a sheet to her. It was too warm of a night for there to be anything heavier than that on the bed, and the linen clung to her body like a second skin.

"I just needed some fresh air," Clint whispered. "I was hoping not to disturb you."

"You didn't disturb me. I was just worried, is all. You should stay in here, don't you think?"

"I'm fine," Clint said as he took off his thin denim jacket and hung his hat on a rack near the door.

But Jolene's eyes were fixed solely upon Clint's gun. The longer she looked at it, the more her face took on the haunted expression that she'd had when looking into Mrs. Parrish's dead eyes. "Do you need to wear that gun all the time? I've about had my fill of them for one day."

Clint walked to a rocking chair that was positioned next to the window looking out at Doctor Branson's place. "Yeah," he said, lowering himself onto the chair. "Me too."

He barely had a chance to get settled before the sound of a creaking bed was followed by light footsteps padding across the floor toward Clint. Jolene stepped in front of him and lowered herself to his eye level.

"Why don't you come to bed? You can see the window just fine from there too, you know."

Clint looked behind him and saw that the bed was indeed aligned with that window. Shaking his head, he turned to look out at the quiet night once again. "I can't sleep."

Moving around so that she was in front of him, Jolene lifted her nightgown so she could straddle him and then sit upon his lap. Wrapping her arms around Clint's neck, she placed her mouth close to his ear and whispered, "Who said anything about sleeping?"

Clint's first reaction was to refuse her advances, but when he started to move her away, Jolene only held on tighter.

"You took care of me," she whispered. "Now, let me take care of you."

"What are you doing?" Clint asked, even as his hands found their way onto her hips.

"You said it yourself. That killer isn't coming back tonight. And even if he did, he doesn't know where we are."

"That doesn't mean he won't try anything. I can't have someone else die because some mad-dog killer wants to get to me."

"We can take care of ourselves, Clint. Someone will come to get you if that man comes into town. Believe me, you're the only one around here who can do anything to stop him and everyone knows it. They'll come running if need be."

Jolene was making a lot of sense. Even though Clint's

mind was still filled plenty of other concerns, he couldn't deny that she felt awfully good writhing slowly in his lap. His hands were already working up and down her legs, feeling the muscles as they slowly shifted beneath her skin.

He started to open his mouth to say something else but was soon cut off by the touch of Jolene's lips against his. She literally took the words right out of him before they could be spoken as her tongue slid gently into his mouth.

The moon wasn't as bright as it had been, but there was enough pale light coming through the window for him to see the impressive curves beneath her nightgown. Jolene's body was solid and well toned. It was the body of a woman who worked for a living and right now, she was working hard to get Clint's mind away from what bothered him.

Needless to say, she was doing a hell of a good job.

Clint watched her face carefully as he let his hands wander over more of her body. Every so often, she would glance out the window, but then her eyes would close as she felt him explore another part of her. Jolene pulled in an anxious breath and grabbed hold of the back of the chair. From there, she arched her back and pressed herself against him even harder until she was rubbing against the bulge at Clint's crotch.

"I want you, Clint," she whispered. "I want you to take me right now."

Never one to refuse a lady, Clint wrapped his arms around her waist and gripped her tightly as he lifted them both off the chair. Jolene's eyes widened with surprise as she looked around to find herself being carried over to the bed.

Rather than lay her down on the mattress, Clint lowered himself onto the edge of the bed so that she was still sitting on his lap. The moment Clint was sitting again, Jolene moved off of him so she could kneel on the floor at the foot of the bed.

She kept her eyes locked onto him while reaching around to unbuckle his gun belt and strip it off of him.

Smiling hungrily, Jolene set the gun belt on the floor and pushed it away from the bed. She then got to work stripping him out of his jeans but was stopped as Clint stood up and did the work himself.

"I can't wait another moment," he said, piling his clothes and boots next to the bed.

Jolene looked down at his erect penis and tugged her nightgown over her head. "I am so glad to hear you say that."

Before Jolene could make another move, Clint sat back down onto the bed and started to lie back. She stopped him by kneeling on the floor once again and lowering her head between his legs. She had his cock in her mouth within the next second and was devouring him like a stick of candy.

Cupping him in one hand, Jolene used her other hand to rub his stomach and chest as her head bobbed up and down. She started to moan as she felt him grow even harder in her mouth. The next thing she felt was Clint's hands urging her to climb onto the bed on top of him.

FORTY-TWO

Jolene crawled on top of Clint, letting her blond hair spill over her shoulders to brush against his chest. Her eyes wandered over his body, taking him in as she spread her legs open to straddle him. When she felt his hands begin to caress her backside, she closed her eyes and worked her hands over his body.

Moving like she was in a dream, she reached down to wrap her hand around the thick shaft of Clint's cock. Jolene then lifted herself up a bit and positioned his erection between her thighs. Slowly, she lowered herself on him and let out a soft groan as she was impaled by him.

"Oh God," she whispered while leaning back and sliding all the way down.

Clint watched every move that she made. Her figure was outlined in the pale light that filtered through the room. Jolene's stomach clenched as she began rocking on top of him, and her large, firm breasts began to sway with the rhythm.

Reaching up to slide his hands over her skin, Clint cupped her breasts and pumped his hips slightly between her legs. He could feel her nipples growing harder as her breaths started to come in short gasps. Before long, Jolene reached up to place her hands over Clint's and arch her back.

She was using her legs now to ride his cock at a quicker pace. Her pussy was slick and Clint's cock eased perfectly in and out of her. Opening her eyes, she looked down at him and smiled before turning to look over her shoulder.

"What's wrong?" Clint asked without letting up on his constant pumping. "What are you looking for?"

She tried to talk but was having trouble forming the words. After pulling in a few deep breaths, she said, "Nothing's wrong. God, this couldn't be any more right. I want you on top of me."

"Really?" Clint's hand moved down along her stomach so he could rub a little circle around her clit. Between the motions of his hips and hers combined with the way he rubbed that sensitive nub of flesh, Clint could feel her body responding almost instantly.

"Y . . . yes," she whispered. "Get on top of me. Fuck me, Clint."

Clint reached up with his other hand to slide his fingers through her hair. He then pulled her down so her face was close to his and she needed to support herself with both hands against the mattress.

"Don't you like this?" he asked.

He could feel that she liked it just fine. Her pussy was getting wetter by the second and she was tightening around him as though she was already about to climax.

"I love it," she breathed. "Right there. Oh God."

Clint's hand had moved from her clit and around to her backside so he could guide her movements to fall in step with his own. Out of the corner of his eye, he could see Jolene reaching down toward the floor.

Casually, Clint grabbed that arm by the elbow and brought it back up to where he could see it. He then threaded his fingers through hers and pumped into her with added vigor.

Jolene clenched her eyes shut and let out a moan of pleasure. She arched her back and allowed her body to move completely on instinct. It now seemed that she was back in control and she thrust her hips back and forth faster and faster once Clint's rigid penis was rubbing her in just the right way.

"Please," she gasped while tugging at his shoulders. "I want you on top of me."

But Clint didn't respond. He was giving into his own instincts for the moment and had just gotten himself to move perfectly in tune with Jolene's thrusting hips. Just when he felt her pussy tightening around him, he pulled her down so she was pressed against him and started to lift himself slightly up to meet her.

Jolene smiled at first but then saw that Clint was trying to get a look at the window behind her. Taking hold of his chin so she could turn his face toward hers, she stared into his eyes and said, "Don't worry about what's out there. Just think about what's in here." With her other hand, she traced a line down Clint's stomach until she brushed her finger between her legs where Clint was entering her. "And what's in here," she added.

Feeling her hand touch him as he entered her was almost enough to send Clint right over the edge. Dropping back onto the mattress, Clint grabbed Jolene by the hips and hung on as she started to ride him even harder.

She let out a moan that filled the entire cabin, mixing with the sound of their sweating flesh coming together. Even though the desert night was cool, beads of perspiration traveled along Jolene's naked skin after the sheer amount of effort she was putting into riding him.

Every so often, she would tug at his shoulders, urging him to get on top of her until she almost seemed ready to beg for him to do so. But Clint wasn't about to move from where he was. The more he resisted, the more Jolene seemed to be driven crazy by it.

And the more Jolene felt him resist, the more she seemed to enjoy the challenge. It got to the point where she saw a smile breaking across Clint's face and she stopped in the middle of what she was doing.

Tossing her hair away from her face, Jolene let out an exhausted breath. "You really like torturing me, don't you?"

"You don't seem to be too upset by it."

She reached down between her legs and rubbed the length of his cock that wasn't inside of her. "I hope you won't keep me waiting for long. You're wearing me out."

Clint took hold of one of her wrists and then the other. When she started to move, he thrust up inside of her a bit more. The pleasure that sent through her caused Jolene to bite her bottom lip and shudder slightly.

"Why do you want me to move so badly?" he asked. "It seems like this is pretty good the way it is."

"I know," she said breathily. "It's just that . . ."

Her words trailed off as Clint gently eased in and out of her while shifting slightly to the side with his hips. That motion caused Jolene to pull in a deep breath and hold it. There was no way for her to hide the fact that her orgasm was almost there.

"Just that what?" Clint asked softly. "Just that you want me on top of you . . ." He pumped up into her, making sure his cock rubbed against her clit.

Jolene was still holding her breath and rocking slightly with her impending climax.

Clint watched her nibble on her lip and sway with the pleasure he was giving her. "Or do you just want to make sure my back's to that window so your friend outside can get a clear shot at me?"

FORTY-THREE

Jolene's eyes snapped open and she let out the breath she'd been holding. Clint was still inside of her, though, and his hands were still firmly clasped around her hips.

As she looked down at him with a mix of shock and urgency creeping onto her face, Clint slid up inside of her until his cock was buried deeply between her legs.

"You started this," Clint said. "Now, all of a sudden, you're looking for a way out?"

Jolene lowered herself on him and let her arm dangle off the side of the mattress. But Clint's arm was just a bit quicker and was able to grab hold of her wrist just tightly enough to stop her.

"It's funny," he said, "how you know about the gun under this bed but didn't seem to know about the shotgun under the counter back at the hotel."

"What shotgun?"

"The one that was under the counter the whole time when that killer was taking shots at us. Or, I should say, taking shots at me." Clint's hands still rested upon Jolene's hips, but he felt that she wasn't trying to get off of him. "The same shotgun that anyone who truly worked at that hotel would have known about."

"Clint, I don't know what you're—"

"Oh, you know damn well what I'm talking about. Have you always worked for him or did he just hire you to set me up?"

Jolene didn't say anything.

"I'll admit you had me going for a while, though," Clint continued. "You came in at just the right time and looked really scared at the hotel."

"I was scared! Galloway almost killed us both. Don't you remember?"

"I do. You want to know what I don't remember?" Clint looked deeply into her eyes and said, "I don't remember ever mentioning Galloway by name."

There was a heavy moment of silence as Jolene started to fidget nervously on top of him.

"And before you tell me that he signed the register," Clint added, "I'll just tell you to save your breath. I already checked the register when I went out for some fresh air a while ago.

"Folks around here seem awfully guarded, but with good reason. You weren't, though, and that kind of struck me as odd this whole time. You were all over me in a way that seemed almost desperate. In fact, I was even wondering if you weren't forced into doing something you didn't want to do."

"That's it," Jolene said, nodding vigorously. "He forced me. I didn't want to do anything. I'm so sorry."

Clint watched her carefully as she spoke. Although she was still naked and on top of him, their bodies were no longer connected. He'd seen to that within the last couple of seconds.

"Sorry?" he asked. "Sorry for not telling me I was in danger or sorry for doing your damnedest to get my back to that window? Or are you just sorry that you can't reach the gun under the bed so you could shoot me yourself?"

Jolene's eyes were locked on him and she slowly shifted

her weight. Some of her hair fell over her face as she came
to a decision at what to do next. Balling up her fist, she
pulled her arm back and dropped it across Clint's throat.
She reached down with her other hand for the gun under
the bed while turning to look toward the window where
Clint had been sitting.

"He's in here!" she shouted. "Hurry!"

FORTY-FOUR

Clint felt her trying to roll off of him, but he kept her in place by getting a firm grip on her arm. Although she was pushing with all of her weight against his throat, he could still pull in enough breath to keep from blacking out too quickly.

A shot exploded into the cabin through the window, shattering the pane. Clint managed to get a look past Jolene as she wriggled on top of him; he saw the glint of moonlight off a rifle on top of the nearest neighboring building.

Another shot came but drilled through the wall at least a foot over Clint's head. When a shot didn't follow that one, Clint knew it was only a matter of time before the cabin's door was kicked in.

Before he could worry about that, Clint needed to deal with the woman who'd turned into a beast on top of him. Jolene's teeth were gritted and that grimace quickly turned into a smile as she finally pulled her other hand up from under the bed.

Sure enough, her fist was closed around a small revolver. She raised herself up and brought the gun around to point at Clint.

"Why all this trouble?" Clint asked, looking directly at Jolene rather than at the gun in her hand.

Jolene smirked and sat upright. Now that she had the upper hand, she didn't seem to mind that she was still bare-breasted and straddling him. In fact, she seemed to enjoy it almost as much as when they'd been making love.

"I've been following you for over a month," she said. "A saloon girl here, a face in the crowd somewhere else, you never noticed. Galloway's had people following you when-ever possible ever since you hurt him. He didn't need to step in himself until we all lost track of you when you crossed into Nevada. And look what happened when he did step in. He makes such a mess that the U.S. marshals come after him."

"Why all the trouble?" Clint repeated. "Couldn't any of you have taken a shot at me along the way?"

"Sure, and we could have gotten gunned down like everyone else who just decides to take a shot at you. Be-sides, that's not what we were paid for. Galloway wanted you followed. That's it. And when he met me here, he told me to move in on you and set you up for his shot. He said that every man had their weakness and that yours is women. He said I could get closer to you than any man without too much trouble."

Shifting her hips so she could rub the dampness be-tween her legs against Clint's skin, she added, "You know something? He was right. It was easy. For a while, I thought killing you was going to be easier than killing that old bitch at the hotel. I did that one for free and handed over that lockbox to Galloway happily. Serves that old bitty right. An unfamiliar woman comes through here and she and everyone in town assumed I was a whore."

"Sounds to me like that's exactly what you are," Clint replied.

Narrowing her eyes to angry slits, Jolene sighted down the barrel of her pistol and squeezed the trigger.

FORTY-FIVE

When the hammer of Jolene's pistol dropped onto an empty chamber, she was the only one who seemed surprised.

"Oh, I forgot to mention," Clint said. "Checking that hotel register wasn't the only thing I did while you were asleep."

"Doesn't matter," Jolene said. "Galloway should be here any moment and I can tell you for certain that you didn't unload his gun."

"Yeah, but now that he's got me dead to rights, what makes you think he'll hesitate to kill you just to clear his path so he can get a shot at me?"

That made Jolene think for a moment, which was all it took before the front door to the cabin was finally kicked in.

Galloway filled the doorway, holding his rifle in a left-handed grip while wildly searching the dark for where Clint was waiting. The moment he saw him, Galloway lifted the rifle and took a quick shot, which caught Jolene through the meat of her right shoulder and knocked her onto the floor.

"God damn you, Adams," Galloway snarled. "I put you through hell and now your reckoning is finally here."

Clint smirked. "Yeah. Too bad you still won't be half the killer you were before I clipped your good trigger finger."

The rage in Galloway's eyes burned so brightly that it almost seemed to cast a red glow to his face. He levered in another round, staring at Clint without trying to hide the madness that had been eating him alive since the time they'd crossed paths in Wescott.

Now that Jolene was off of him, Clint rolled off the bed and dove for the pile of clothes he'd stacked there. He dug beneath the clothes until he got to his boots. His hand immediately found the knife he kept there. It was the same blade that had nearly crippled Eclipse.

Galloway's rifle exploded through the shack, punching a hole through the mattress. Clint had already rolled further away from the bed; when he came to a stop, his arm was cocked back close to his ear.

Both men's eyes met in the space of that single instant.

Galloway's expression was full of equal measures of insanity and victory. The latter disappeared when Clint snapped his arm forward and sent the blade spinning through the air to slam into Galloway's throat.

The rifle slid from Galloway's hands, but he didn't seem to notice. He was too busy reaching up for the knife handle that protruded from his neck just below his chin. Dropping to his knees, Galloway kept his eyes on Clint until he finally fell over onto his side.

Clint got up and started to walk toward his gun belt but saw that Galloway was the only other person in the cabin. A trail of blood led outside to the spot where Jolene's horse used to be. Letting out a calming breath, Clint went to his clothes and slid them on before strapping the modified Colt back around his waist.

Galloway lay on the floor with the tip of his own knife protruding from the back of his neck. His eyes were still on the spot where Clint had been and he was reaching out with his right hand.

Clint spotted something that caught his eye. It was a small book protruding from Galloway's pocket. Picking it up, he flipped through the book and found a list of places Clint had been and the dates that he'd been there. After tucking the book into his own pocket, Clint looked back down at Galloway.

The hatred that had taken the place of his missing trigger finger was still visible on Galloway's features, as was the insanity that had driven him to such lengths over a debt that Clint hadn't even known about.

Clint couldn't help but laugh a bit under his breath. "The funny part is that you were still one hell of a killer without that finger. At least you got the reckoning you were after."

With that, Clint left the cabin and headed for Doctor Branson's office. There was already a small group of locals gathering outside.

"What happened?" asked a man dressed in a nightshirt and boots. "We heard gunshots."

"There's a wanted man lying dead in that cabin," Clint explained. "Take him to Carson City and collect the price that's on his head. Use the money to pay for a lawman around here. Or just bury the poor bastard. I don't care which."

"What about you?" the man asked.

Clint didn't even break stride. "I'm going to check on my horse."

The man looked confused as he poked his nose into the cabin. "Where's the whore who rented this place?" he asked. "Will she be coming back?"

"I don't reckon she will," Clint replied. "Hopefully she'll be smart enough to find another way to earn a living."

Watch for

RING OF FIRE

281st novel in the exciting GUNSMITH series
from Jove

Coming in May!

J. R. ROBERTS

THE GUNSMITH

GIANT ACTION! GIANT ADVENTURE!

THE GUNSMITH GIANT

GIANT WESTERNS FEATURING THE GUNSMITH

THE GHOST OF BILLY THE KID
0-515-13622-0

LITTLE SURESHOT AND THE WILD WEST SHOW
0-515-13851-7

AVAILABLE WHEREVER BOOKS ARE SOLD OR AT
WWW.PENGUIN.COM

J799